A SHIFTER'S CLAIM

PALE MOONLIGHT, BOOK 4

MARIE JOHNSTON

LE PUBLISHING

A shifter without a mate is a shifter without a mind.

It's been five years since Shilo's mate walked out on her and she's been just a little, *tiny* bit unstable, a feeling that isn't helped by the impending fight with a neighboring colony. She might not be all there, but even a crazed shifter knows waking up in a stranger's bed hours from home to find the contacts from her pack murdered means she's in trouble.

Aimless and restless and unconcerned with anything beyond his next one-night stand, Waylon agrees to act as bodyguard for some shifter pack liaison embroiled in a power struggle. What could it hurt? He's been aching for five years, and maybe this assignment will take his mind off all he's lost. But when he meets his client, his world stops. It's *her*. His mate. The one he left.

Thanks to their history, he can't just walk away and leave her as a target. Thanks to her instability, she can't go home without backup. If either wants to survive the bloody present, both will have to set aside their heartbreaking past and fight for their uncertain future.

For my readers. In case no one's told you today, you are worth it.

For new release updates, chapter sneak peeks, and exclusive quarterly short stories, sign up for Marie's newsletter and receive download links for the book that started it all, Fever Claim, and three short stories of characters from the series.

CHAPTER 1

*S*hilo scrambled back, searching the scene as horror filled her. With a sated sexual appetite, common sense returned. Blood marred the sheets, splintered wood littered the floor, and a naked man lay in a crumpled heap at the base of the bed.

Did I kill him?

She remembered most of it. The flirting, the smiles, the lingering touches. The invite to a party at his place. She'd sent her envoy home against their wishes and hopped in with… What was his name?

She also recalled thinking how five years ago, this guy wouldn't have turned her head. He was too clean-cut, too arrogant, too lanky, and dressed way too nice with his tapered jeans, loafers, and snappy polo.

Once, she'd searched for quiet confidence, shaggy hair, a muscular build, and clothing swiped from a pile on the floor to fill that empty ache she suffered each day.

Now it seemed any male who could survive her would do.

She prodded her fangs, then winced. The blood-tinged tips of her fingernails caught her eye.

She glanced down at the prone body. What was his name again?

Michael? Micah? Dave?

She took in a calming breath, a steady inhale to fill her lungs. Hold two seconds, release. Okay, it wasn't unusual for her kind to randomly and indiscreetly fuck without having to swap business cards. They were shifters with primal urges.

But she couldn't lie to herself. Her urges were getting more than primal. They bordered on rebellious and in her world, that way lay a shortened lifespan.

What had set her off this time?

You must be on your best behavior to secure the technology contract with the Covet pack. They've formed solid relations with the humans and can help us upgrade every facet of the colony, from cable TV to security cameras in the surrounding woods.

Her mother had uttered one wrong word in that sentence. *Must.*

Shilo pushed her long hair off her face and stared at the man. She'd gone home with another human again? Was he breathing?

He was familiar. That's right. He was the computer programmer who was best buds forever with Langdon Covet. Her mouth curled into a sneer.

The programmer had been sweet and flirtatious. Langdon had disgusted her so entirely that she'd put her entire colony at risk by going home with the computer guy. All because Langdon had so smugly assumed she should be enamored with him.

Sorry, she'd only lost her head over one male before, and all she'd gotten in return was his abandonment.

Realization dawned that she was baring her fangs just

thinking about the one that got away. Ran away was more like it. Coward.

She sniffled and batted at a renegade tear. All these years and she still lost salt water to a worthless male.

Glancing down at herself, she frowned. Naked. Her clothes were strewn around the unfamiliar room. The place was nice, except for the destroyed nightstand. It hadn't been able to tolerate the full strength of her hold during an orgasm. She had to hand it to the human, he'd been good at least. His sheets had been clean—once they'd finally made it to the bed—and they hadn't made her sneeze from chemical-laden cologne.

So I've killed a decent guy. Perfect.

The man groaned.

With a gasp, she knelt by his side. He was breathing, and if she hadn't been frozen in her what-about-me fear, she would've sensed his heartbeat earlier. Looking him over, she could've wept from the relief crashing through her. His wounds were superficial, and while one or two scratches might scar, was it arrogant to think he might enjoy the thought that he'd made a girl lose her mind in bed?

No one could know that her mind was unstable on its own.

"Hey." She gently shook him. "How you feeling?"

He blinked his eyes open and groaned again. Like her, he didn't have a stitch of clothing on. The only thing he wore was her love bites.

She worried her lower lip. One bite showed two deeper indents from her fangs. She hadn't revealed them last night, had she?

"Whoa." His voice was hoarse. Hers would've been, too, but she was a shifter and had already healed. "You are a wild one in bed." He squinted around the disheveled room. "And out of bed."

3

You don't know the half of it.

She gave what she hoped was a demure smile and not one that rivaled the big, bad wolf. "You made me that way," she lied.

He rolled to his back and sat up. She rested on her heels and reached for her cream-colored shirt, confirming with a quick inspection that it was blood free. Her nudity didn't bother her, but she didn't want him to think she was interested in more. She needed to get home. Her parents had probably waited for hours for her to come home with updates. As the Ironhorse pack's ambassador and future colony leader, it was her duty to report to the current leaders.

Twenty-six years old, and she had a curfew like a human child.

"I've gotta get home," she said with another smile that was supposed to look regretful. "Thanks for the fun night. Can I grab you a water and toast before I go?"

He should have something with protein, too. She found her charcoal-gray slacks and the red heels she'd worn to the meeting. Stepping into the pants, she spied her underwear and grabbed it. Those were shoved into her tiny pants pocket. Where was her bra? Why'd she have to dress in the most inconvenient clothing for these pack meetings?

Professional wear was not conducive to one-night stands, but her colony was trying hard to be taken seriously in the shifter world. It was that or get incorporated into another colony's leadership. She couldn't be the cog that failed centuries of rule. And she wouldn't turn her home over to slimy Langdon Covet.

The man touched the tender scratches along his side. Snippets of the night were coming back to her. She'd raked her nails down his chest and thrown him to the ground when he'd taken too long bringing her to climax.

He cocked his head, a sexy grin spreading across his face. "You don't have to rush off so soon, do you?"

A bloom of heat curled through her belly, but no. She had the upper hand over her instincts for now and she planned to hold on to the reins as long as possible. "Work beckons. Hang tight, I'll grab you some juice."

With her heels in one hand, she found his kitchen easily enough. This wasn't the first unfamiliar place she'd woken up in. Large windows lit the place up with late summer sunshine, and the cedar-toned hardwood floor was smooth and level under her bare feet. The unnamed man was doing well for himself. Langdon was paying him well to supply the Covet pack.

Vile shifter.

She couldn't prove it, only that Langdon repulsed her. He'd always seemed to have his target set on her, even when she'd been with Way—

Why today? Why was she thinking about the worthless male who'd obliterated her heart today?

Duh. Because she wouldn't be here if it weren't for him. She wouldn't be worrying about her sanity or her future with the pack. She wouldn't be eyeballing males she'd grown up with, wondering which one was going to be tasked with hunting her down once she finally succumbed to the call of the wild. At least she'd be too crazed to care when it happened.

She set her mouth in a line and opened the stainless steel fridge door and found orange juice. Perfect. Ooh, a packet with cheese and a hardboiled egg. Judging from Nameless's muscular body, he ate a high-protein diet. She poured juice and took the glass and the food to her hookup.

He'd moved to the bed and had a gray satin sheet pulled over his groin, but from his expression, he was open to moving it if she asked.

"I'll just set these here." She deposited the protein and drink into his hands since the nightstand was defunct. Stooping, she picked up her black clutch, which held her phone and some cash. "Take care."

He frowned and moved like he was going to stand. "Shilo, how are you getting home?"

Stiffening, she quickly relaxed her body language. This was nothing more than casual sex, and the better impression she left on the human, the fewer rumors would spread. "I have my ways. Don't worry about me."

Once she stepped outside, she could figure out where she was in Freemont and make her way to one of her pack's safe houses. Just like she'd done before.

"But—" Bare feet shuffled behind her. She rolled her eyes since her back was to him. "I can give you a lift."

And show a man who worked closely with her colony's biggest problem this century where her people were stationed in Freemont? Or worse, have him find out she lived in the middle of nowhere and give a human a reason to start asking questions? Rural was an understatement and Langdon Covet kept them as isolated as possible.

Her colony was parked in the foothills far north of Freemont, the closest metropolis. It took a full tank of gas to travel to and from there. Langdon's fledgling but surprisingly fortified colony was on the main road between her home and Freemont. A strategic decision, in her opinion. One that explained why there were so many transportation break- downs and missing shipments of supplies between home and Freemont.

But her parents had to prove it and Shilo had to help. And that'd been her task. Set up contracts, prove Langdon violated them, get him with the law. Instead, she'd probably risked angering a male who seemed obsessed with her by going home with one of his clients.

Five years ago, she'd have never— Well, it didn't matter now. Five years ago her destined mate had walked away, and now everyone assumed she had more time before an epic personality fail.

"I don't need a ride. Thanks for the offer." She breezed out his front door. She peered left, then right. Identical entrances were on either side of her. This must be a condo or townhouse. He had neighbors. Good. Then he wouldn't rush after her until he got dressed, and she'd be long gone by then.

Her surroundings didn't help her determine where in Freemont she was. She must've been prisoner to her needs last night to not notice where she'd been going after the meeting.

There was a swell of traffic off to her left. She'd walk there and call a ride service. As long as her phone wasn't dead. Charlie and Cass would loan her a ride from their used-car lot and Shilo would coordinate payment for the ride. It was becoming a routine.

She should really establish a friend with benefits, someone she could hit up for regular sex who was good enough to wear her out and fool her mind into thinking she had a mate who hadn't abandoned her. It seemed to help the bitterness and resentment, the constant desire to break pack rules and go against long-established laws. Maybe that'd prevent her from pushing her limits.

If her family discovered she was on the brink of going rogue, they'd lock her up and find a mate for her ASAP. Shilo's stomach twisted at the thought of mating another, even to save her life. To be dependent on another to such an extent that she'd be destroyed when he left?

Been there, still doing that.

And she didn't care about a loveless bond to save her own life, she wasn't willing to give up her independence. Not yet. She'd been making do. She could get through this until...

Until what was the big question haunting her, but her instinct said to keep fighting.

A gas station was six blocks away. When she got there, she pulled up an app and set up a ride. The fare to Charlie and Cass's, or C&C as she liked to call them, wouldn't cost much. The highlight of her morning was getting to see them.

C&C were both lifelong friends, and they were the only ones who had witnessed her lowest point without attributing her behavior to *his* leaving, even if it had been a direct cause. They'd never said she was better off without him or that she deserved better. They'd just let her cry and despair in private, and they hadn't questioned her when she'd moved on.

It'd been hard when they'd decided to move to Freemont, but pack members living in another town wasn't unusual, as long as their allegiance remained to their pack. Her friends had felt their career was being stifled in Ironhorse Falls and that they could better serve the colony as contacts in Freemont. If Shilo didn't help her colony get with the times, C&C wouldn't be the only shifters leaving for better options.

As she sat on the curb and waited, she finger-combed her hair and ignored the curiosity of passersby. Her gray slacks were dusty and wrinkled, but she hadn't shredded her shirt getting naked last night, so things could be worse.

Her Uber pulled up and once she was inside she finally scrolled through her messages.

Mother: Where. Are. You.

Father: At least an update?

Mother: Sweet mother earth, not again. What are you thinking?

Father: You okay?

Langdon: How was he?

Shilo glared at the last message. How could arrogance travel through printed words like that? Langdon probably took credit for what's-his-name. He'd hinted that they could keep their options open if they combined their packs, if she mated Langdon.

Nope.

Mating Langdon seemed like a good choice in smart packaging. He was handsome, rich, positioned in an ideal location for her people. But her gut had screamed at her when he'd first alluded to it. She'd be a pawn, a puppet, and, probably, a prisoner. Langdon held all the power. Her people were strong and resourceful, but without ready access to supplies and technology, they'd lose in a direct battle for supremacy. Their people had a relatively new government tasked with leading them in the new world, but shifters still defaulted to a "might is right" mentality. She had no qualms that their government would uphold a hostile takeover by the Covets. Over the years, he'd set her people up to prove they weren't strong enough to lead themselves.

The car pulled up in front of C&C's sizable two-story home. They lived on the outskirts of town, where the lots were measured in acres and the woods crowded behind them. As ideal for suburban shifters as it could get. Shilo paid and got out. The car was pulling away as the sense of wrongness hit her.

She scanned the neighborhood. One neighbor cruised around his lot on a green riding lawn mower. Another was getting the jump on winter and stringing his Christmas lights up. July *was* nicer weather for the task. Kids' laughter echoed from nearby lots, but C&C's place was quiet. And a tint of blood laced the air.

Shilo inched toward the door, her stomach plummeting with each step. The blood got stronger. No birds sang from around the house.

Her throat constricted. She didn't sense anyone nearby, but Charlie's and Cass's smells were too strong for them to be okay.

She didn't bother to call out. It'd alert the neighbors and she had to make everything look normal for the humans.

The door was unlocked. She pushed inside, letting the pristine white door swing open. A sob caught in her throat.

A wall of death slammed into her.

Dragging in a shallow breath, Shilo forced herself to step inside and close the door behind her. One foot in front of the other, she walked out of the foyer and into the main room. The seventy-two-inch TV was off, and in the leather loveseat in front of the screen sat her dearest friends, side by side, their heads held in their lifeless hands in their laps.

CHAPTER 2

*a*hard rap echoed through the room as a deep bass said, "You've got a phone call."

Waylon pried his eyes open. He'd been in the back room of the club since his shift had ended. What time was it?

A blond head bobbed at his crotch, but his cock barely felt a tickle. It was taking more and more to get him off lately. And give the woman an award, she was trying hard, but he was saved from the *it's not you, it's me* speech by his boss's knock. If it weren't important, his boss wouldn't have interrupted.

Gently, he lifted away the girl's head. "Hey, I've gotta go."

His cock popped out of her mouth. Her eyes were still glazed in passion and he mourned not being able to finish her off, but he had a phone call.

She moved to prowl up his body, but with his half-limp dick, she'd get nowhere. And he had a phone call.

"Business. Not personal. I've gotta go." He rolled off the chair and separated the clothing scattered on the floor. He found his blue T-shirt and jeans, the standard bartender uniform at Pale Moonlight. Sometimes he changed up his shirt color. He glanced at his phone. It was midmorning and damn, he had a lot of missed calls.

He frowned at the name. M&S Security. Right, he'd told them he'd do some freelance security bullshit for them.

Once he was dressed, he ran his hands through his shoulder-length hair. He should get it cut, but who cared? Before he left, he turned to the woman he'd spent the whole night with. This part never got less awkward. At least she was also a shifter and knew the deal. Meet, fuck, leave. They weren't mates, they were just answering the call of the wild.

But he felt like he owed her more than a fist bump.

"Thanks." That was hardly more.

She lifted a light brow as she shimmied into her leggings. "Welcome."

Good. They were done then. He breezed out and strode down the hallway. A few groans echoed from the rooms he passed. It wasn't unusual for them to be occupied until noon. The rest of the bar was empty. The wooden booths and tables were wiped and chairs were stacked so the floor could get cleaned before another night of shifter partying and debauchery.

Christian was behind the spotless bar, the recessed lights gleaming off his dark scalp. He didn't look up, just pointed to the old-fashioned landline sitting off its base.

He grabbed the receiver. "Waylon here."

"It's Armana Miller. I have a job for you."

He was grateful she cut to the chase. He didn't need a lecture on not being available when he'd only given them a *sure, I can help out once in a while* agreement. Lowering the mouthpiece, he addressed Christian. "Armana's got an assignment. Can you spare me?"

Christian snorted as he combed through register printouts. "Absolutely."

Waylon smirked. He suspected Christian and his old

bartending buddy Jace had begged Armana to give him work to do. Too much time on his hands, too much fucking—as if there was such a thing—and lately, too much attitude. Getting out of the bar and all the pheromones from coupling might be a good idea. Instead of losing himself in it like he used to, it was making him bitter.

"Lay it on me, Armana."

"I have a female who needs an escort from Freemont to her home colony."

He was going to be a chauffeur?

Armana continued. "She's at the Guardian lodge right now. She was in town on business, mediating relations between her pack and another, when her contacts in town were murdered. The Guardians are investigating, but her pack fears for her safe return."

A little more interesting. But he didn't care to drive all over the boondocks. It'd remind him too much of home and he'd moved to West Creek and gotten a job at Pale Moonlight to forget where he'd grown up and who he'd left behind.

"All right. Who is she and where do I take her?"

"Why don't you meet me at the lodge and we'll go over everything in person."

Right. A murder was involved and she didn't want to talk over the phone.

"Be there in ten." He hung up.

"Aren't you going to pack anything?" Christian asked in his deep baritone, with a tone that said *you should go prepared*.

"Nah. It's just some down and back. If they wanted fancy, they wouldn't have hired me."

Christian gave him a steady look. As a pack leader of misfits, he didn't like being disobeyed, even if he didn't give an outright command. But if Waylon could follow pack orders, he wouldn't be bartending at a shifter hookup joint.

Waylon knocked on the bar's surface before turning to leave. "See you later."

Outside, he squinted into the sun and hugged the shade of the building to weave around back where his Jeep was. It'd seen better days—both him and the vehicle. The faded black Jeep was weathered and a rust spot was eating away at a wheel well, but it still ran. Kind of like him. They were still going, just not as sporty as before.

Maybe he should run home and pack a few things.

Nah. With pack business and murders, the female he was transporting had too much on her mind to even notice him.

The drive to the Guardian's lodge was beautiful as always, and as always, he tried not to notice. Lush trees, space for wolves to run, and the smell of the great outdoors would only remind him of just the beginning of what he'd lost. How long had it been since he'd run his wolf?

Years.

The massive log structure sat at the end of a winding drive. The architecture of the place was genius. The generous windows reflected the woods back to the viewer like built-in camouflage. It was two stories with a full basement. Around it, cabins dotted the woods for Guardians and their families to live in.

He rubbed the sudden ache in his chest. The families out here were tight, had been through thick and thin, and that was not envy burning a hole through his gut.

Parking by the entrance, he jogged inside. Armana's human mate, Gray, met him at the door.

Waylon had only met the guy when they'd come into the bar to talk with him, but he liked Gray's relaxed demeanor. The human had nothing to prove and his delight in his new life was palpable. Again, not envy.

"Waylon, thanks for coming so soon."

The corner of Waylon's mouth ticked up. Thanks for

coming so soon after they'd been trying to reach him for hours. Diplomatic.

"Armana's with the client now. I'll let them explain everything."

Waylon arched a brow. The client was doing the talking. She must have status.

He followed Gray down a long hallway with coded locked doors. Scents assaulted him and he tried to parse through them as he walked, like there was a hidden treasure tickling his nose. One door was hanging open and Gray turned inside.

Waylon rounded the doorway and froze, his boots scratching to a halt against the floor when his gaze landed on the client.

No. It couldn't be. Anyone but her.

His heart pounded, a deafening cacophony in his ears.

Wide brown eyes switched from shock to full hostility. She stood so fast she knocked her chair over. "No. I will not work with him."

The venom in her tone knocked his sense back. That voice, so much disdain for him, like her mother, like her father, like half the town he'd grown up in.

Aware of Armana's and Gray's growing alarm, he adopted a smile he didn't feel and drawled, "After all this time, is that how you greet your mate?"

CHAPTER 3

"We never mated, you coward."

Waylon's head started to pound. He should've eaten something before he'd left. And her scent. It was different. Not like before, but if he sifted through the lingering death attached to her, he could smell—his fangs throbbed.

"Ugh." Shilo spat on the floor, though the move was only for show. She probably considered herself too classy to spit for real. "You smell like cheap sex. Get out of here. You're an insult."

Armana's back hit her chair, her gaze wary. Gray hugged the wall.

His anger rose hot and swift. *He* smelled like sex? "As opposed to the expensive kind you just had?"

A quick flash of regret filled her expression and she switched her attention to Armana. "I'm sorry. I can't work with him."

"Ditto," he said from between clenched teeth.

Armana glanced between them, then at Gray. She nodded

and rose. "Okay. I can see there is bad blood between you two. We'll accompany you back—"

Gray was shaking his head. "We're both already tasked with security detail. But I'm sure the Guardians can put Ms. Ironhorse up for another night while we find someone else."

He should leave. Storm right out. Let someone else worry about her privileged ass.

But his stubborn feet wouldn't move. "Who do you need to be protected from?" He managed to say the words with a sneer.

"It quit being your business when you left," she shot back.

"Waylon, you may go," Armana said firmly. "We'll compensate you for your time."

"No. You hired me." What was he saying? "Christian already gave me the time off."

Shilo crossed her arms. Unfortunately, it drew his attention to her breasts. He'd never seen a pair that measured up to hers. "No."

"I don't know if that's a good idea, Waylon," Armana said.

He straightened, wishing for the first time he'd done something other than roll away from a blow job and come straight here. "I can be professional." He cocked a brow. Would Shilo rise to the bait?

Shilo tipped her head. "Since when?"

"Princess, you know I won't let anyone hurt you."

She scowled at the pet name. Her family wasn't rich, but they'd pampered her, and everyone in the colony knew it—but not like he knew it.

Shilo managed to look down her nose at him despite the five inches he had on her. "Only you're allowed to hurt me?"

Ouch. His chest ached at the memory of their last words to each other.

Why am I not good enough for you? I thought you loved me. He'd lived for only her.

Only cowards walk away.

Those weeks—hell, months—before he'd left... A guy could only tolerate so much for the female he loved when she accepted everyone's dismal treatment of him.

"Want to get into old arguments here, princess?" He crossed to the chair beside Armana and pulled it out. Settling in, he said, "We can see whose side they take."

Shilo's pink lips flattened, and if he hadn't had shifter senses, he wouldn't have noticed her shoulders sink a millimeter. That's what he thought. He'd left her, his mate. But there'd been a reason.

She stared at him, her eyes cunning. He had no idea what she planned, but he gestured to her fallen chair behind her.

Armana studied the both of them. Gray righted the chair as if sensing Armana's grudging acceptance. The couple was mated—happily, even—so he must've.

Again, not envy Waylon felt at all.

Armana sighed. "I'm sorry, Ms. Ironhorse. I wish I had more options for you, but Waylon has excellent recommendations, and I hate to use this, but if you two really are mates, he has a serious advantage over those who may be after you."

"Wait," Waylon said. "May be?"

Shilo opened her mouth, but Armana spoke first, thankfully. "You must be familiar with the Ironhorse Falls colony." Was he ever. "Are you familiar with the Passage Lake colony?"

"The place run by arrogant pricks who found a reason to stop and search me every time I drove through their place?" He'd secretly hoped a bunch of Ironhorse pack mates would crop up in Passage Lake, just to see Shilo's parents' reactions. "They're only lawful enough to stay under the Synod's radar." Their government was swift in reaction, but they tried to let pack relations work first.

"Ms. Ironhorse," Armana continued, "is the Ironhorse Falls colony ambassador and she's been negotiating with Langdon Covet, the Passage Lake leader."

He could see that. Shilo liked to work both sides. Never be the bad guy. It was the reason her parents worried about her taking over. She wasn't ruthless enough, and they hadn't thought he had the grit, or could earn the respect, to be by her side. But the other packs in the Ironhorse Falls colony, and the shifters in her own pack, adored her. Her wit, humor, and strength—and her looks—had won them over.

Shilo opened her mouth like she was about to say something, but then she averted her gaze.

Armana waited a heartbeat before she finished. "The most recent meeting was in Freemont last night. Ordinarily, Ms. Ironhorse spends the night in town." His heart hammered in his ears. That was code for "went home with someone." His mate. Just like he spent most nights with Not His Mate. "The couple who organizes her transportation home was found dead this morning, and Ms. Ironhorse and her family don't believe it's a coincidence."

What was the likelihood the couple had been murdered by the shifters after Shilo—

"It was Charlie and Cass, Waylon." She heaved out a sob and sucked air right back in.

Cold washed over him. He hadn't heard those names in years, but... Damn. Charlie and Cass? He'd been at their mating ceremony. With Shilo. They'd all hung out. Those two were the only shifters in Ironhorse Falls he'd called friends.

He fisted his hands on his legs. The stars of his only good memories from before he'd moved to West Creek were gone. "How were they killed?"

"Beheaded," Shilo answered. A muscle ticked in her jaw.

"It was like they were mesmerized and someone just sliced their throats, let them bleed out, then..." She touched a knuckle to her lips and drew a fortifying breath. "The murderer put their heads in their laps."

"And you think Langdon fucking Covet did this?"

"I think he's behind it, yes. And I couldn't drive home through Covet territory all by myself."

"What were they doing in Freemont?" When he'd left Ironhorse Falls, his friends had still lived there.

"They moved a few years ago. Sales in Ironhorse Falls dwindled too much in the last decade. In Freemont, the market was wide open and residents weren't as sluggish about upgrading vehicles." She shrugged, grief etched in her face. "When I started doing more and more business in Freemont, they loaned me a different car for each trip back. Sometimes I could make it through Passage Lake before any Covets realized it was me."

A wise precaution. Shilo had never been stupid. Stubborn, yes. Frustrating. But not stupid. If she'd lacked intelligence, maybe she would've come after him. Instead, she knew what everyone else knew. He wasn't good enough for her.

Armana cleared her throat. "Our original plan was to hire you to escort her home and provide security for all future envoys, but if you could just accompany her home—"

"I'm all in," he growled. "Charlie and Cass were my friends, too."

Armana and Gray glanced at Shilo.

She narrowed her eyes on him and was quiet for several moments. "Fine. But you can't interfere with my work."

"When have I ever?"

Her mouth clamped shut. When they'd been together, he'd bent over backward to make sure she knew he loved her for who she was, not what she was. No one could accuse him of taking advantage of her. They had anyway.

Armana and Gray exchanged unreadable looks. As a human mate, Gray couldn't mind speak with his mate or any other shifters, no matter how close he was, but it didn't appear to matter. The two were so in sync they could tell what the other was thinking.

It used to be like that with Shilo. Or he'd thought so. He'd been wrong in the end.

The ache in his chest was back. Probably heartburn, from all that breakfast he hadn't eaten.

Fuck, what had he agreed to?

WHAT HAD SHE AGREED TO? Shilo glanced at Armana, willing the shifter to be the sensible one and announce this was a terrible idea and someone else should accompany her to Ironhorse Falls. Preferably a female.

Waylon striding through the door, with his typical *I don't care* expression that she knew was a lie—or so she had once thought. The way he'd left her had proved her wrong. He looked good, as always. Almost better because he was extra broody and disheveled and that had always been her favorite thing about him. But he smelled atrocious. She hadn't been exaggerating. Sex oozed from every pore, and not the kind with flowers, cards, and whispered promises. Fast. Hard. Anonymous.

Shilo had the sudden urge to sniff herself.

Expensive sex. Did it matter? It had still been fast, hard, and anonymous.

Her righteous anger was dying down and she couldn't let that happen. Memories assaulted her, tightening her chest. Telling him their mutual friends had been killed brought with it the happier memories of how they'd all known each other. She and Waylon had been the first ones C&C had told about their bonding date, and before that how they were fated mates taking it slowly. Shilo had laughed with Waylon. Taking things slow? It was unusual to find mates so early in life. Shilo was only thirty-three, barely an adult in many shifters' eyes. Waylon, they guessed, was around her age. He'd confessed one dark night that he didn't know what year he'd been born, that he'd extrapolated from his estimated age when he'd been found in the woods as a child.

Compassion threatened to rise, but no. Not for him. Not anymore.

Armana rattled off instructions to Waylon about contacting her regularly so she could update the Guardians. When she was done, Waylon pushed back, the flex in his biceps hooking Shilo's attention. She ripped her gaze away.

If he had so much as sent her a text or an email, or hell, a candygram, since he'd walked out on her—on *them*—she might be willing to soften. But he hadn't and she wouldn't. If Waylon couldn't handle the courtship, then he couldn't handle a full bond. She had even more responsibilities than before, and she was barely hanging on to her dedication to her pack. Her mental state would snap if he left a second time and then she'd be mindlessly homicidal. Since fate hated her, the shifter sent to kill her would probably be Waylon.

"My Jeep's outside, princess."

Ugh! That name. She lived in a modest house in a failing community, but she'd been born with more than Waylon had arrived at their colony with. "Princess" ought to be the name of the chasm separating them.

"You still have that old thing?" She rose and followed him out. Armana and Gray were on their heels, probably trying to decide how bad of an idea this was.

"No, I went and bought a brand new one off the lot." He

didn't spare her a glance. "Or better yet, one of my pack members gifted me with a brand new one, fully loaded."

Ass. Her childless aunt and uncle had bought her one car and now Waylon thought it was a regular occurrence.

"You have another pack?" she asked, adopting a haughty tone. Her parents had kicked him out of Ironhorse as soon as they'd seen her sobbing on the floor.

"I'm not some rogue piece of shit."

She stiffened and glanced around like a hit squad was going to materialize out of the walls and get her. She maintained pack law, as much of a struggle as it got to be some days. Disobeying her parents, who happened to be not only pack leaders, but also colony leaders, was still within bounds. Passive-aggressive rebellion. If it'd been anyone but her, there'd have been some serious discipline doled out. For now, Shilo was just getting her mother's exasperated sigh.

"I never said you were," she muttered.

"But you never said I wasn't," he retorted.

She stopped in the middle of the hallway. He walked a few steps before he caved and stopped, too. "If this is going to work, we can't constantly be egging each other on. I don't like you." The lie stuck in her throat. "You don't like me." All her previous heartbreak threatened to well up. "We're working together, nothing more. Quit calling me princess and I'll call you Mr. Wolf."

"Waylon. Just call me Waylon."

He'd never shunned his last name before. They hadn't known his real one when he'd been found, and Waylon had adopted the last name of the reclusive shifter who'd taken him in.

Armana and Gray walked them the rest of the way out, much like nervous parents sending their daughter off with a date they didn't know well. Or vice versa. Shilo could only

23

guess when she was going to snap and try to rip Waylon limb from limb.

Oddly, she was feeling less ragey today than she had in a while. Perhaps it was her efforts last night. Surely it had nothing to do with Waylon.

Her breath caught at the sight of Waylon's beat-up, rusting Jeep. Why that thing? They'd had sex in it. Long talks. Laughter.

The memory of his prideful smile as he'd showed it off after buying it from C&C's used-car lot in Ironhorse Falls played through her mind, bringing all the emotions of the day with it. She and Waylon had made love in it and on it so many times—and she could remember them all if she tried.

"Damn," she said.

"Sorry it's not a Lexus." He misread her dismay and that was just fine with her. He'd probably written over all their times together with someone else.

She ran her tongue down a fang. It wasn't her business. Just like her dating life wasn't his.

"Unless you can read minds, don't assume you know what I'm thinking." And it really was a good thing he couldn't. He'd see flashes of their frantic fucking in the back, or the time he'd laid her across the passenger seat, with the console prodding her back, and stood in the open door to take her hard.

That'd been one of her favorites.

These thoughts were going to drive her crazy. "If we leave now, we can get back before nightfall." It was a good six-hour trip and the late summer light faded by eight p.m. They'd get back in plenty of time, depending on the delay Passage Lake would inevitably make.

"Not so fast, princess." She bristled at his pet name, but he didn't notice or, more likely, didn't care. "I need to swing by my place and pack an overnight bag. And I gotta eat or I'm going to get hangry."

"Oh no," she deadpanned. "You're going to get crankier than you are now? How will I ever tell?"

He shot her a sidelong look and walked around to the driver's side. There had been a time when she'd almost never opened her own door, especially not when they were riding together. Looks like that time had passed. She crawled in and was swamped by his scent. Along with the more familiar woodsy musk of her mate was the cloying scent of alcohol and pheromones. She breathed in. Not just his own pine smell, but that of the crowd at the bar. All those shifters seeking to work off the high sex drive that nature had bestowed upon them were like walking perfume spritzers, spattering their lust-filled scent on everyone they crossed paths with.

Unlike many of them, she knew how cruel nature was. Sex with a mate was phenomenal, addicting, so good it made it possible to imagine eternity with only one person.

Since Waylon had walked out, sex now left her merely physically satisfied if she was lucky, but emotionally empty regardless.

They didn't speak on the way to his place. She couldn't think about spending not only today with him, but who knew how many days until the mystery of her friends' deaths was solved. Concentrating instead on who could've pulled off a double beheading kept her occupied until Waylon parked in front of a square steel building. Windows dotted the side and the parking lot was empty except for two other vehicles in no better shape than Waylon's.

"Is this where you live?" She frowned at their surroundings. A tire store was across the street, a gas station at the end of the block, and the closest building was a double row of storage units with standard-sized garage doors. This neighborhood didn't scream residential.

"Did you think I was holed up at the Ritz?"

"Freemont doesn't have a Ritz, jackass."

The corner of his mouth quirked up. Her insult lacked conviction, and she hadn't meant it to. She crossed her arms and rested her head against the back of the seat. "Take your time."

"I'm not going to leave my charge by herself in a parking lot within the first half hour of being a bodyguard. Come on up." He got out and slammed the door.

Her stomach clenched. Go into his place? See how he'd been living without her? And witness how he was doing just fine?

She couldn't sense any instability in him. And while she was staggering under the grief from her friends' deaths, Waylon acted like the same male she'd once loved.

Jack. Ass.

Growling under her breath, she climbed out and followed him. He unlocked the glass entrance door and held it open long enough for her to get close enough and grab it before he took the metal flight of stairs up two at a time.

The door thudded shut and clicked solidly in place. She was locked in with him.

The bottom floor had been sectioned into offices. A long hallway ran to the exit at the other end of the building. Doors and the occasional business logo broke up the monotony of white walls.

As she took the stairs, one at a time, she eyed the directory of businesses. *West Creek Parole Office. Check In Cash Out Money Services. Hail?—I Don't Bail Insurance Company.*

"Interesting neighbors," she commented.

Waylon's voice came from above. "They're quiet during the day."

She crested the top. One massive wall blocked off the second level. Waylon unlocked a deadbolt in the heavy gray metal door. Once he swung the door open, he paused like he was going to usher her in first but thought better of it and breezed inside, pushing the door open far enough that she could catch it before it shut her out.

The inside was...not surprising.

Bare metal walls, exposed beams in the ceiling, and ratty linoleum came together in a lackluster industrial feel. A kitchen lined one wall with a counter to separate it from the rest of the...apartment? A bed with rumpled gunmetal sheets was at the end of the place and a walled-off square that must be a bathroom made up the only interior wall off the kitchen.

A sagging punching bag hung from a beam in the middle of the room.

"Your interior decorator should be fired." She crossed to perch on a barstool at the counter as he ignored her and headed toward his bed. She had to put her back to him. Waylon by a bed was too much for her psyche to process today. The urge to scent the place was irresistible, but the lack of a female smell was surprising. He slept and ate here, got a workout in, and that was it. He kept the sex out of his home.

She wasn't sure what to think of that.

Fabric rustled and drawers opened and closed. He was packing. His muscles were probably flexing and bunching as he bent and stretched to pack a bag, but she refused to watch him.

"Are you going to shower before we go?" she asked. On the other hand, the stench of sex on him was a turnoff. *Should* be a turnoff. Maybe wasn't as much as it should be.

"After you. If I have to smell that rich bastard on you, you can smell..."

She barked out a laugh to cover her relief that he couldn't

seem to remember his partner's name either. "Trixie? Melinda? Davina?"

"I'm not sure we got that far," he grumbled like he wasn't happy about it.

"Eau de rich bastard it is then." She stood. "Oh wait, you needed to eat." Her stomach rumbled. Had she not eaten yet, either?

"We'll grab something on the way." He was going for the door, but she went to his fridge. A package with the butt of a loaf of bread was wadded in the corner. Moldy cheese slices were next to it, and in the middle was a carton of milk that could probably walk itself to the sink. Takeout Chinese containers and pizza boxes littered the other shelves.

Waylon was the best cook she knew. Was he boycotting cooking?

"Good thing shifters don't get clogged arteries." She stared at the pizza boxes. The pizzeria in Ironhorse Falls had shut down. She'd love to sink her fangs into a greasy slice.

"Are you hungry or horny?" Waylon's voice broke in. "It was always hard to tell with you."

She couldn't be angry. He was right. She liked food as much she liked sex. "Starving. Mia's Pizza closed. Let's grab pizza."

"Why the fuck did they close?" Waylon's jaw was slack, like hearing Mia's was no more made the world a darker place. And Shilo would agree.

"Their shipments were always delayed to the point that their goods were spoiled by the time they arrived. Most businesses are having those issues in Ironhorse Falls."

"Covet pack?"

She nodded. "We can't prove it. Flat tires. Blown engines. They get hopelessly lost in the country. Lately, orders have been getting canceled or amounts get messed up to the point of breaking the bank, and since Langdon Covet is a tech genius, you can see why it's been so hard."

His jaw tensed, the muscle she used to nibble jumping. "We'd better get going."

She took a fortifying breath. Ironhorse Falls and all of its packs were in trouble. Waylon was back in her life and she was taking him back into the lion's den. At least they could be civil. She could keep her distance. As long as he kept his.

CHAPTER 4

*W*aylon's hand gripped the wheel. Any harder and he'd warp it. They'd been driving three hours, hitting the road as soon as they finished eating.

Shilo hadn't held back with her pizza. Her appetite had always been sexy as hell, but her pizza deprivation had ended with gusto. She'd moaned over the cheese, licked the grease off her lips, and rolled her eyes in ecstasy. He'd only been able to choke down two slices before he'd abruptly pushed back from the table and stalked to the Jeep with the rest of his box.

And the way Shilo had smirked—she'd done it on purpose. The little minx.

He would've laughed at his own reaction if he hadn't been so uncomfortably hard. But with Passage Lake looming in less than an hour, he was winning the battle against his hormones. According to Shilo, a lot of peculiarities happened around the colony.

Trees crowded in on each side of the highway. The road lacked a decent shoulder, dropping to steep ditches or tree-plugged countryside almost immediately. The sun was still out, gradually sinking behind the tops of the branches.

As much as he dreaded stepping foot back in Ironhorse Falls territory, the land called to him. It was in his blood and the longer he drove, the more his inner beast celebrated being home.

His wolf preened around Shilo, too. It was like the handful of years had drained away and he wanted to dive right back into the months before he'd left. Shilo's parents had at least been civil. He and Shilo had been dreaming—no, planning—their future together.

Now he was heading back where he said he'd never go back, and for a female he'd sworn off of. Damn his mating instinct that wouldn't let him walk away when she was in danger.

He repressed a shiver as shadowy fingers danced down his spine. Narrowing his eyes, he scanned the trees.

Shilo had been scrolling through her phone to avoid him while sitting an excruciating six inches away. She clicked her phone off and glanced around.

"What?" she asked.

"I don't know. Just something's off."

She didn't dismiss his intuition but intensified her gaze, searching their surroundings.

The Jeep faltered, like the pistons quit firing for a heart-beat. No check-engine light came on, but Waylon bet the closer to Passage Lake he got, the more engine "problems" he'd have.

He didn't believe in coincidences. "They have someone who can tamper with vehicles."

"We thought of that, but it'd be a helluva talent to be able to create different issues in different vehicles."

He bit the corner of his tongue at the mention of talent.

Most shifters had something extra, a little gift that made life easier, whether it was among their own kind or to blend in with humans. He had next to nothing, and it was another strike against him and why he was such an undesirable mate for Shilo.

"I'm sure there's more than one," he said.

"That's not possible. I mean, our gifts are usually so different."

"Is it that unlikely when we're so isolated that our packs interbreed and continue to live among each other?" It'd only been this century that his people had ventured into cities. The packs closer to each other or living within larger human populations had different stories. But Ironhorse Falls and Passage Lake were lone wolves as far as colonies went. There was enough turnover in residents to prevent inbreeding, but it wasn't like Freemont, where several packs mingled in the area.

"But to have the power to tamper with vehicles, sometimes semis? That's a feat."

"Yep." Didn't mean it wasn't possible. "They have strong bloodlines."

Shilo must've agreed. Her brows were furrowed as she considered what he'd said. Hadn't they ever thought of it before?

They drove several more minutes without issue. Then the hairs on the back of his neck stood up.

"It's gonna happen again," he said. He didn't know how he knew, he just did.

Shilo stiffened and craned her neck out the back window.

The engine stuttered, hiccupped, and went back to normal.

Her dark eyes went from the speedometer to him. "How did you know?"

"I feel...something." It wasn't unfamiliar. He'd always

dealt with tingly sensations over the course of his life. But they'd never amounted to anything before.

"Like you *feel* it feel it?" she asked. "Like it's your thing?"

He shrugged. "Maybe?"

"Huh."

Had he always chalked it up to coincidence? Just one of those feelings and never exploring it further? Or was it Shilo back in his life that made this different?

They topped a hill. Streetlights dotted the countryside. On the descent, they passed a sign that read *Passage Lake, pop. 2810*. That was for humans who happened out this far for hunting and fishing. Shifters couldn't keep them out completely, nor did they want to as they were a source of potential mates, among other things.

The trees thinned only slightly, towering taller and healthier than the clustered woods. The underbrush wasn't as thick thanks to the locals keeping it down, whether by mowing or running their wolves.

A gas station bordered each side of town. Like clockwork, his engine started shuddering and ticking the closer he got to the gas station. The check-engine light popped on. Surprise.

"Look at that." Shilo shook her head. She'd tied her long brown hair back on itself. However she did it was like magic to him, but somehow she used her own long hair to tie back the rest. "If it were me in one of C&C's vehicles, what would've happened? I bet the Covets gathered details on all the cars they sold."

Would they remember his vehicle? Probably not. He'd hardly traveled from the colony; it'd been as close to a home as he ever recalled. When he'd been with Shilo, he'd had no reason to leave. And then he had.

Guess he wouldn't go back quite yet. He had to see what Langdon Covet wanted to do with him.

The Jeep's power drained the closer they got. He idled

into the lot. A grizzled shifter swaggered out of the open garage door on the side of the gas station. The male's shrewd gaze burrowed through the windshield. The guy's brow creased three times over when his gaze landed on Shilo.

Her chin was already kicked up, her shoulders square as she got out. "Paulie. The weirdest thing—we're having engine trouble." Sarcasm laced her tone.

Paulie wasn't familiar to him. And the waves of increasing hostility coming off the shifter didn't reassure him that they'd get out of here without some drama.

"Shilo, we're always glad to help you." But the man's dark gaze said he wasn't up to helping Waylon.

Waylon wasn't into playing games and didn't care to be at the mercy of any Covet, and this male had the look of a Covet. Dark hair, amber eyes, the swagger of someone who ruled the town, or whose family did.

Waylon tapped his hood, catching Paulie's gaze. "Why don't you tell your pack to quit fucking with my vehicle and we'll get outta here."

Shilo gave him a *what are you doing?* look.

Paulie's eyes darkened a few shades. "What the hell are you talking about?"

"We both know, so let's not pretend." Waylon believed what he was saying so much, there was no worry of Paulie smelling a lie and calling his bluff. "I can shift and go for a nice run while waiting for you to work out that nothing's really wrong. If I run across any shifters, we can discuss abilities. What are the odds I'll find one with some mechanical talent?" Waylon tipped his head forward. "Other than you, of course."

"Who the hell are you?" Paulie's elbows flared out as he strutted closer. In his grimy overalls, he looked like an anaconda imitating a cobra. Waylon crossed his arms and leaned against the hood.

"Someone who isn't going to play Covet games. Now, Shilo and I are getting back inside. If my Jeep doesn't work, I might just have to mention to my buddies that there're these weird occurrences centered around Passage Lake." Waylon shrugged. "My buddies, they're Guardians. And they owe me."

The police force of their kind had come to Waylon for several favors. But they'd never tried to recruit him. Another group of people who didn't think he belonged with them. Whatever. He wasn't cop material anyway.

"Shilo." Waylon pushed off and went back to the driver's door. He'd been careful how he said her name. If he was too forceful, it'd undermine her authority. But if he deferred to her too much, Paulie wouldn't take him seriously.

Shilo didn't hesitate. It would've taken the threat out of everything he'd said. If the Ironhorse Falls ambassador trusted him, he was someone to be listened to.

Paulie glared at them. "We don't take to strangers making accusations."

Waylon opened his door and leaned on it. "Well, then. Why don't we go have a beer, chitchat, and then I'll repeat what I just said. Would that unhurt your feelings?"

Nostrils flared. The shifter morphed from anaconda to bull ready to charge. "You can chitchat with our leader."

A door slammed. Shilo was in the Jeep. Waylon cocked a brow at Paulie and got in. The engine turned over and settled into a steady purr. Wouldn't ya know it.

Waylon pulled away and it took more restraint than it should have not to roll the window down and drive through Passage Lake with his middle finger in the air.

He was already risking enough calling them on their game.

"I can't believe you did that," Shilo muttered.

"It wasn't doing any good keeping your suspicions to yourselves."

"It's not your place to decide—"

"Oh, princess, it is. They were gonna take us in that little gas station, have a little talk, get as much dirt on our business as possible, and then let us go. That's after they ran my plates and bugged my vehicle or whatever they have up their sleeve."

Shilo's eyes flared when he mentioned bug. "Oh my God. I never thought of that."

"They might not have the capability, but you said Langdon's a tech guy. I'm sure he has lots of toys Ironhorse Falls doesn't know about."

"I'm certain he's a hacker."

"Or someone from their pack is." What would Langdon Covet's talent be? And why was he targeting Ironhorse Falls so hard?

"He works with a lot of humans. Perhaps he hires out and covers it up with the other contractors."

The edgy feeling Passage Lake gave Waylon made him think anything was possible. They were almost through the small colony, nearing the gas station bordering the other side. He was still moving slow, obeying the speed limit, when a shadowy figure sauntered into the middle of the road.

There was something familiar about the guy. He was about Waylon's height, dark brown hair cropped close to his scalp. Longer hair fell over eyes that glittered in the Jeep's headlights like the predator he was. Unlike Paulie's overalls, this guy wore black slacks, black shoes that gleamed in the fading light, and a yellow polo with a logo Waylon couldn't make out yet.

"Langdon." Shilo didn't sound overly fond of the man. She wasn't swayed by good looks and smooth words—Waylon was her mate after all—but he still worried. One look at

Langdon and damn. Waylon worried *he'd* be swayed by the guy's charm.

He left off the gas. There was no reason for him to stop, but in this case, flying past the leader of the colony was blatantly rude, and he'd done enough damage already.

Stopping next to Langdon, Waylon took his time rolling down the window. As the glass lowered, the scent of freshly felled pine, arrogance, and power permeated the Jeep. And an underlying sense of familiarity. Had they met before? In the days when Waylon had been just a colony degenerate and Langdon a budding dictator?

Langdon looked past Waylon like he wasn't there. "Shilo. Is everything okay? Paulie said you might be in trouble."

Shilo wasn't fazed. "What would make Paulie think I can't take of myself?"

Langdon bowed his head, his expression appropriately chagrined. "My apologies. He's almost as protective of you as his own pack."

Just what Waylon had thought. Smooth.

Waylon gave him the best bored look he could muster. "That's cleared up then. We'll be going."

He eased off the brake, but Langdon's strong hand clamped down on the doorframe. "I don't believe we've met. You're not from one of the Ironhorse Falls packs."

Definitely not the Ironhorse pack itself. Shilo's parents had made it clear that would never happen.

"I'm not," Waylon agreed. "Have a good night."

He let off the brake and was careful with the gas pedal. Giving Langdon a brush off showed he both wasn't intimidated by Langdon and had nothing to hide; squealing tires as he sped away would make it seem like they were scared.

Shilo waited until he raised the window before she hissed, "My God, Waylon. You probably set back pack relations five years."

How fitting. That was how long he'd been gone. "Like I said, whatever you've been doing hasn't been working."

"That's not your call. You're my bodyguard, not an ambassador, not a pack leader, not our spokesman. Shut up and look tough."

He ground his teeth together. She spoke the truth, and he wasn't too proud to admit he might have stepped outside his bounds in his efforts to help. But hadn't that been the issue? No matter how he tried to help, no one wanted him around —Shilo most of all.

SHILO PREPARED what she was going to say to her parents when they arrived. They'd want to be updated on the meeting, C&C's deaths, and her bodyguard situation. Only they didn't yet know who her bodyguard was.

They wouldn't be happy it was Waylon, and that was a major understatement.

Waylon hadn't spoken since she'd lashed out at him. She'd just intended to make a point, not insult him, but like in the weeks before he'd left, she couldn't say anything right around him.

As they approached Ironhorse Falls, she pondered where he'd sleep. She still lived with her parents. The house was big enough, but Waylon managed to make a room feel small and the tension between him, her, and them would add extra complications.

He could never play nice. If he scented a hint of animosity, he made it his mission to earn it since he could never change it. Zero attempt at congeniality. Then Waylon acted like others disliking him was inevitable. No wonder Cass and Charlie had been their only friends as a couple. Charlie had had the gift of gab and could sell fleas to a wolf.

He makes you happy, Cass had said once when Shilo asked her why she was one of the few who tolerated him. *And he's a good guy with a lot of walls in place.*

But Shilo's days of weathering Waylon's behavior because of his upbringing as the unwanted foster pup were over. He was an adult now and as an adult, he'd proved how unreliable and hard-hearted he was.

She stared out the window. Familiar terrain passed but the soaring evergreens and rolling hills didn't fill her with the peace they normally did. She had to face her parents about why she'd been stuck in Freemont and how it had brought Waylon back into her life. And that would be after Waylon appeared on their doorstep. It would be an uphill battle.

Moments like these, she felt like a teenager again.

Maybe she should move out. It was just easier not to. Usually.

For the foreseeable future, it was going to be more difficult.

"Still live at home?" Waylon must be having the same thoughts.

"Yep."

She lived on the far edge of town. Unlike Langdon, her family didn't stalk the perimeter to interrogate visitors. The road to her home wound through tall pines and past the other small houses and cabins that Ironhorse Falls' residents favored. Her colony wasn't situated around a lake like Passage Lake. Homes here dotted the hills and were built out of logs, stone, and some timber. Her parents had forbidden the packs to congregate and build around each other. Instead, their pack members' homes were interspersed among each other, and neighborhoods weren't pack oriented.

The colony bore the name of Shilo's pack, the pack the

leaders of the colony had originated from, but her parents made an extra effort to treat all packs as equals. The Ironhorse pack was the largest, but there were four other packs in her colony.

Waylon made the last turn to her place.

That was why she hadn't moved. Her home was constructed of logs, but the exterior walls up to the alpine roof were made of local stone. The mason had been gifted with a sense of how the rock fit together to maximize stability and aesthetics.

Since she was an only child and her parents wanted her around forever, they'd designed the place to have the ability to be broken up like a townhome. She had one wing, while they resided in the other.

Waylon would have to stay in her wing, and thank the sweet Mother she had more than one bedroom.

"Park in the back," she said. Daylight had faded and if luck was on her side, they had gotten through Ironhorse Falls without Waylon's Jeep being recognized. But that didn't mean she wanted to display his vehicle for all her neighbors to see.

The closest neighbor was a half mile away, and while they were considerate of personal property, they had good eyesight and ran their wolves every day. The beat-up Jeep would stand out and shifters had great memories.

He took the drive around the back and parked by the door to her wing. The fragrant junipers under her window would conceal his Jeep until they could get it inside the garage.

"Let's get this over with." Waylon got out and grabbed his duffel from the back.

Shilo gathered the few items she'd brought and trudged to the back door. She opened it to find her mother staring back at her.

Mother was an older version of her. Shilo had gotten her dad's pert nose instead of her mom's patrician one, but they shared the same dark eyes, high cheekbones, and sloping forehead. Mother kept her hair in a long braid and each decade brought more gray. She never shared her true age, but Shilo guessed she was younger than the gray indicated. Like maybe a few centuries old. Father liked to joke that she was the cougar going after a younger man. He was only sixty-two.

"Did a Covet give you any troub—" Waylon's scent must've hit Mother before he appeared behind Shilo in the doorway. Mother's fangs bared. "What is *he* doing here?"

"Funny coincidence. The guy they hired to guard me happened to be Waylon." Shilo pushed past Mother. It'd been a long day. She and Waylon had an agreement and her parents would have to deal.

"Who hired him?" Mother blocked the doorway. Waylon was stuck outside, the strap of his bag digging into a broad shoulder. His face was as neutral as he could probably get it, but emotion roiled in his eyes.

He was as upset as Mother.

"I can't talk to you about the day if you don't let him in." When Mother didn't move, Shilo elaborated. "He's been hired to protect me. We're not back together. End of story."

Mother arched a dark brow. Shilo understood the unspoken question. How could two destined mates claim not to be together when they showed up together?

The familiar drag on her heart happened when "destined mates" fluttered through her mind. Being back home, with the male she'd once planned her entire life around, was messing with her tired mind, and her lonely soul.

Shilo started for the conference room situated in the middle of the house. The family room was under the peaked roof, the conference room on the other side of it, toward the back of the house.

Her heels clicked on the hardwood floor, announcing her presence long before she reached the conference room. Father was already there.

He didn't smile or nod when she entered. No, he knew Waylon was right behind her.

Father stood at the table, his arms braced on the top. His jet-black hair was pulled back in a queue and he wore one of the old Western-style shirts he favored with metal snaps and a collar too large to be cool in any time period other than the 1970s. Shilo liked to tease him that he was decades behind the times. He shot back that his style had stalled when he'd met her mother.

Waylon crossed to a brown padded seat. He dropped his bag, sat, and folded his hands across his belly.

Mother entered, exchanged a loaded look with Father, and sat down as far away from Waylon as possible. Shilo took the chair situated between them both, across from Father. The door stayed open; no one else was in the house. The varnished wood walls of the room closed in on Shilo and her lack of sleep reared its head.

"If you'd come home last night, this wouldn't have happened," Father began.

She cut in. "I shouldn't have to censor my life because Langdon is trying to take over our colony." It would've been a whole lot easier to cater to her increased urges if she could come and go freely, without another colony altogether interfering.

Father's lips pursed. Mother dropped her head. Because she was right. The way Waylon had handled business at Passage Lake hadn't only upset Shilo because she feared he'd made relations worse. No, worse was that doing so had shown her how much her family had been placating

Langdon Covet to keep things from reaching a boiling point.

Shilo continued. "It wasn't just last night. Someone's been watching me, watching Ironhorse Falls residents when they go to the city. They targeted Charlie and Cass—they *planned* it in order to strand me in Freemont." She hunched against the seat. "Strand all of us at random times to make us feel powerless."

Mother jutted her chin toward Waylon, who quietly watched the conversation. "And how'd *he* get involved?"

Shilo shrugged. "The security agency I hired is new, with only a few employees. Waylon was who they had free. We discussed the issues between us, but he agreed to take my case."

"He's taking our money to protect you," Mother sneered.

Waylon leaned forward, his hands resting on the cool, smooth surface of the table. "She's not paying *me*. She's paying M&S Security, who I work for."

Best not to mention she was his first assignment.

"You can't think it's a good idea," Father said.

"We don't." Shilo slipped back to the subtlety she'd used when she and Waylon were dating. Dropping tiny details to show her parents they were united. "But like I said, we discussed it."

"There was no one else to take her case," Waylon interjected.

Shilo glared at him. Why'd he have to push it past the line?

Father's look was openly hostile. "We can find someone from one of our packs to provide security for Shilo."

"Go ahead." Waylon stood and the meeting room shrank to half its size. "I'm sure Langdon Covet would love to hear that Shilo can't make her own decisions—and that she's afraid to travel by herself. He'll be thrilled when he learns

43

that we're supposed to be mates and you fired me. There's literally no one else who can protect her life like I can. But hey, I'm sure he won't take strategic advantage by blocking something as simple as wifi, right? You can figure the rest out."

Father's expression wavered. Waylon was blunt, but he was right. Langdon would find a way to capitalize on this situation.

"You aren't part of Ironhorse Falls anymore," Mother said.

"I never was." Waylon crossed to the door and gave each of her parents a pointed look. "You made sure I knew it was on paper only, and the rest of town followed your example."

He was about to leave when Shilo barked, "Stop. For fuck's sake, the decision is made. Grab your bag and find the spare room. We can reconnoiter in the morning." The urge to snarl at her parents was getting harder to fight. A sick part of her brain urged her to lash out, to make the fight physical. The call to press Waylon to the wall and show him why he couldn't leave was just as disturbing.

Six hours in the Jeep with the mate who'd dumped her and she'd been mellow. Five minutes at home and her rogue was showing.

But she could hide it a little longer.

Her temples pounded and her fangs throbbed. She needed a good night's sleep. It'd be better in the morning. "It's been a long day, but before I retire for the night, Waylon had an interesting observation in Passage Lake."

Waylon came back in while she explained their encounters with Paulie and Langdon. He didn't sit, but hefted his duffel and waited.

"So," Shilo wrapped up, "it's something to think about. Langdon didn't like being challenged about it and he didn't like Waylon. We need to take a page from his playbook and use it to our advantage. Now, I've gotta get to bed."

She rose and walked out. Waylon was on her heels. His presence irritated her as much as it was a balm to her rising rage. Until she reached the landing of the wooden staircase that arched to her room. It was really a suite that took up the entire top floor of the wing. The bottom level had the spare bedroom, kitchenette, sitting area, and guest bathroom.

"I've never seen you talk to your parents like that," Waylon said quietly so their voices wouldn't carry down the hall.

Her crankiness bested her. "Yeah, well, I changed after you left."

"Too bad it wasn't before," he muttered and stalked down the hall to disappear into the guest room.

Her mind wanted to return to old arguments. Why she hadn't stood up to her parents. Why she hadn't asked for his mark. Why they'd been together for years without going through the bonding ceremony.

But those arguments were best left in the past. How she acted wasn't his business anymore. He just had to keep her alive.

CHAPTER 5

*S*taring at his black boots wasn't getting him anywhere. He'd risen with the sun, having fallen asleep as soon as his head hit the pillow. With his job—former job—he'd slept during the day and worked the evening until close, then hit the back room with a willing female or two.

But yesterday, he'd not only gotten to bed late, but he'd also been mentally exhausted. Hours and hours with the female he'd sworn off.

There was something different about her. Everything. She dressed classier, though her rumpled top and slacks were the only outfit he'd seen her in since they'd parted. Her attitude wasn't as subdued as five years ago—her temper was quicker to rise and the way she'd addressed her parents had shocked him. That wasn't his Shilo, who played the middle ground like she was rooted in it.

He switched his gaze to the ceiling. There were no footsteps, no running water, and no sounds of an awake Shilo. She used to be up with the sun; morning runs were her wolf's favorite.

Her personality had changed, and her habits must've as well. If she was anything like him, staving off the loneliness was most commonly done after nightfall.

He stared at the floor. Being here was... He'd love to pretend the last five years hadn't happened, but it was the weeks before that, the night before, that he couldn't ignore.

You'd give your life to a worthless mate?

I love him, Mother. We're fated.

Then you cannot be our legacy. You cannot take over for us if you bond to him.

Waiting for Shilo's adamant refusal to bow to her parents' threats had slaughtered him. Because it hadn't come.

We'll wait. They'll soften.

What if they don't? he'd asked.

We'll still be together.

Riding the middle like always. Ironhorse Falls' ambassador. Waylon snorted and shot a look at the ceiling. All quiet.

When was she going to fucking wake up? He was starving.

She had a small kitchen; hopefully she had food. Sitting here was a test in madness, trying to ignore memories of them together that were prompted by every object he looked at. The bed he sat on? He couldn't count how many times they'd made love on it. The dresser? He'd taken her up against it and repaired the gouges in the drywall afterward. The tiny bathroom he used when she took her epically long baths? She'd jumped him shaving one time.

The kitchen wouldn't be safe either. The dozens of times they'd laughed at the counter. The night Charlie had announced over a game of cards that he and Cass wanted them at their bonding ceremony. And, of course, the sex.

He'd taught Shilo to cook. She'd been so coddled she

couldn't boil water. But his time in the isolated cabin with Uncle Wolf had taught him to be self-reliant.

Uncle Wolf. A mystery male to the entire colony and to Waylon himself, despite being raised by the old codger.

Waylon scrubbed his face and stood. He'd been so young when he was brought here by a shifter who'd found him eating a rabbit carcass in the woods in his human form, his only possession a note with a name on it. Shuffled from house to house, the families barely able to tolerate his nearly feral behavior, until he'd landed at Uncle Wolf's.

Another thing he'd lost before he left. Uncle Wolf had been gone for days. Waylon had gone out to the isolated cabin to check on him each day until he returned. And he had. He'd died on the doorstep from wounds that had refused to heal. Silver toxicity. Feet away from the salt that could've saved his life.

Waylon should've stuck around and waited instead of staying at Shilo's. He should've found out how Uncle Wolf had been injured, but the male would've come back from the dead to haunt him for interfering. He'd been that private.

Waylon shook his head. He'd be sobbing in his OJ if he kept this line of thinking up.

In the kitchen he didn't find as much food as he'd hoped.

"What the hell does she eat?" Two gulps of juice were left in the bottle. No milk. No leftovers. The condiments were all different colors and shades than they were supposed to be. He opened the freezer door and his stomach rumbled. What could he make out of a pound of hamburger and old peas? Rummaging through the cupboards turned up spice containers that probably hadn't been opened since he'd left, penne, and a can of mushrooms that expired next month.

The makeshift hash was over half gone before he quit eating and saved the rest for Shilo. She might turn her little button nose up at it, but he couldn't bring himself to eat it all.

He'd have to get his own groceries later so he wouldn't be accused of freeloading.

She still wasn't awake.

He wandered through her home but stayed on the main level. It looked almost the same. Each and every knickknack he'd gotten her was gone. Packed away or thrown away? Too bad. A couple of Uncle Wolf's animal carvings had been so delicate and lifelike, Waylon had expected them to walk away. The carvings Waylon had attempted himself were lackluster, but she'd proudly displayed them on the bookshelves in her bedroom. Bet they were gone, too.

After a few minutes, he'd seen every inch accessible to him. He was staying far away from her bedroom. Might as well watch TV.

He sank into the plush deep-purple couch and turned it on. Static roared through the room.

"Fuck." He hit button after button. Finally, he got it muted and crawled behind the television. The only wire hooked into it came from a DVD player. He couldn't find a coax cable, a Roku, a satellite connection, nothing. She hadn't even bothered to hook up an antenna.

Her sweet-clover scent swamped him before she spoke. "Getting a signal of any kind has become impossible. We'll be completely cut off soon."

She was at the base of the stairs, facing the room he was in. She must've showered last night; he hadn't heard the water running. The navy-blue leggings she wore matched her baggy graphic tee with a picture of the Eiffel Tower. She should look refreshed, but her eyes were as solemn as the dark circles under them.

Was there something going on with her, or was it the stress of the previous day? "Is that what the negotiations were about the other day?"

She nodded and crossed her arms like she was cold. It was

at least seventy in the house. "We're playing it off like we're just trying to get fiber optic cable. If we can arrange to dig in the line for that, we can figure out what's going on with our DSL and telephone lines."

"But an antenna doesn't work."

"It was always spotty out here."

"More coincidences."

"I know" was all she said.

Asking her if everything was okay wasn't an option. She wasn't going to open up to him and it wasn't his place. "There's some hamburger...stuff...in the fridge."

Her eyes lit up. "You cooked?" She didn't wait for an answer but spun around and hunted his food.

He went after her only because he had to know what she had planned for the day. He was dressed in jeans with only a hole over each knee and a black T-shirt. Eh, should be good enough for what she'd have going on.

When he rounded the wall to the kitchen, he caught her trashing the rest of his food. She looked over her shoulder. "I guess I'm not that hungry."

He'd be offended, but her complexion had paled. "That pizza not sitting well?"

"No. I think my midnight snack was off." She dropped the lid on the trash and set the container down. "I guess I should get some decent food. I have to talk to Mother and Father before they meet with the other pack leaders. I'm sure they'll want to share what Covet's been up to, and about...you."

Yesterday, she'd been full of fire, today he couldn't see more than an ember of her energy. "I'll be your shadow."

"All right. I'll get dressed then."

She came down minutes later in gray slacks and a black silk top. For a pack meeting?

She was trying to act the part of future colony leader. Waylon smacked against the bitter taste in his mouth and followed her to the same meeting room he'd been in last night.

He expected more out of the update with her parents. Drama. Glares. Outright hostility. But Shilene and Weatherly Ironhorse must've decided that he was worth less now than he had been before and it was best to treat him as if he didn't exist. Posting himself at the doorway, he listened as Shilo briefed them in more detail about how talks had gone with Langdon.

From her report, the Covet shifter was suave. He'd treated Shilo as if he was their biggest proponent in technology upgrades. He claimed he was willing to meet with the company about where to dig the line and generously offered to let Ironhorse Falls piggyback off of what Covet already had. How convenient for Langdon.

When discussion about the Guardians taking over the murder investigation died down, Waylon spoke, knowing he was the last person the Ironhorses wanted to hear from. "The Covet shifters think of Shilo as theirs."

All three stared at him.

"Langdon thinks he's being charming," Shilo said.

Waylon shook his head. "It's more than that. The way Paulie behaved when he saw me wasn't just aggression over another male challenging his authority on his turf, it was also about a male being with you. Langdon checking on you before we left town was more than a wellness check, or a display of power. His focus was on you."

"You're more attuned to Shilo." Weatherly glanced at him and looked away. A dismissal. "That's why you think that."

Waylon dragged in a suffering breath. "Maybe because I'm more attuned to her, I can tell."

Shilo licked her lips, avoiding his gaze. "It's been his acquaintances that I've gone home with the last couple of times. I doubt he'd be plotting a claim on me without trying to cockblock them."

As hard as it was to talk about Shilo's sex life with other males, he mulled it over. "Do they seem convenient? The first few meetings in Freemont, did you find partners on your own, then suddenly, there were guys with stamina hanging around?"

Shilene sat back and crossed her arms. Motherly anger that a male would orchestrate her daughter's sex life carved into her expression. "Shilo?"

"Well, last night was his IT connection. Before that…" She thought for a moment. A crease formed in her satin skin and she chewed her lip.

Waylon couldn't help his smugness. She was having a hard time remembering. But like him, she probably remembered each one of their times together.

"I think…" Shilo said. "Yeah, I partied with Langdon's old college buddy. Another human. And before that I think I might've been introduced to one of his construction suppliers."

Shilene *tsked*. "Why couldn't you just come home and use one of your regulars?"

"Because they're getting clingy," Shilo snapped. "And I shouldn't have to worry about getting used by who I take to bed."

It was increasingly difficult to play impervious. Regulars? Memories of snide gazes and curled lips assaulted him. Ironhorse Falls was full of males who had thought Shilo should give up on him. They'd joked about keeping them in mind when she got sick of him, or when she realized Waylon wasn't enough. How many times had Shilo talked him out of jumping the bastards?

Turns out she really had kept them in mind. And he hated himself for it.

"Shilo's right," he forced himself to say. "When's the next meeting?"

"Langdon's going to know who you are by then." Weatherly's gaze took on disgust. "I'd love to vouch for every resident of Ironhorse Falls, but gossip finds its way to Passage Lake."

"Two days," Shilo answered. "In Freemont."

Waylon needed to start planning now. "Does the pack give you trouble on the way to the meeting?"

She thought for a moment. "Only when I'm not alone. I've brought the librarian to Freemont before and we were stopped. Then one time, the elementary and high school principals accompanied me."

Waylon didn't know who any of them were. He'd set eyes on Shilo during the one year he'd attempted school, and all other shifters had faded away. Uncle Wolf had offered to teach him what he needed to know, and after experiencing how much time class wasted, Waylon had agreed. Uncle Wolf had looked like he should be holding up a thumb and hitchhiking across the nation with his scruffy face and faded, grungy clothing. But his intelligence had been unparalleled, and only Waylon knew that.

Too bad his cabin hadn't met typical standards. Uncle Wolf's place had lacked heat or an indoor bathroom. Waylon still thanked the inventors of modern plumbing every time he used a urinal and had the pleasure of washing his hands afterward.

"Last year, the colony journalist came with," Shilo said. "I was stopped with each of them. Paulie flirted with the librarian, which I think she pretended to like to keep from causing trouble. Peter, the journalist, got questioned a little more."

"How'd they stop you? Car trouble?" Waylon asked.

Shilo chewed her bottom lip as she remembered. "A check-engine light one time. The gas light. I didn't think anything of it the first few times. They'd chitchat, ask some nosy questions, then send us on our way. And yes, when I was with a male, we'd be delayed longer."

"What made them back off?" Waylon asked. Was she involved with any of the males?

"At the time, I thought it was because they were just being Covet, but now that I think about it, the males I was with were mated and we had no romantic ties. The Covets could've smelled their family on them and left us alone." She chuckled. "Peter probably smelled like spit-up. He told new-baby stories the whole way."

Peter was already mated with kids? He was younger than Waylon and they'd both amicably ignored each other the entire time they were growing up. Unlike several others, both young and old, Peter hadn't felt it was necessary to point out that Waylon didn't have a place in the colony.

When they'd found him as a speechless child in the woods, no one had claimed him. The only possible colonies he could've been from were Passage Lake or Ironhorse Falls. Neither had claimed him, and none of the packs had ponied up and allowed him in. Ironhorse pack had finally given in.

It was like he exuded a repellent for everyone in the colony that had rescued him. Somehow word of him had filtered to Uncle Wolf, and the Ironhorse pack had gladly sent Waylon to live deep in the woods with him. Until Waylon met Shilo, he couldn't figure out why they'd bothered to pluck him out of the woods.

And since the packs in Ironhorse Falls had wanted to pretend he didn't exist, he'd happily ignored them. No use wasting the effort to play nice when the residents found him useless.

He had two days before the meeting in Freemont. There was little to plan for, but Waylon formulated a strategy. "We'll be open about who I am and what I'm around for.

Totally open. Shifters took out C&C, so Shilo might be in danger. But here's what we do: we play up our history." He switched his gaze from Weatherly to Shilene, then Shilo. "You don't like me, but you trust me to keep her safe. We play up that you can't stand me. Shilo and I aren't together anymore for reasons, and we play up the separation, the feelings, the bitterness. Don't hold back."

"Are you sure about that?" Shilo asked.

"Hey, I'm just a bartender who needs extra cash—that'll be my angle. Maybe they'll underestimate me, try to get me out of the way, or buy me off. Whatever they choose will tell us something."

Shilene's lips pursed. Her chin automatically lifted in that superior way she adopted around him. But her words surprised him. "If they ignore you, they'll think Shilo's vulnerable. If they try to get you out of the way, their intentions for Ironhorse Falls are more aggressive than we feared. And if they buy you off, they'll confirm all our suspicions about the orders and shipments. I wouldn't be surprised if Langdon paid good money for a direct ear into this town."

"Those humans he tossed in Shilo's way," Weatherly agreed. "Right. I'll call the pack leaders in to discuss our needs for the next meet up. Our residents are getting antsy with the lack of outside communication."

Waylon crossed his arms and didn't move. He would be sitting in on the meeting, just like this one. They were stuck with him, and that fabulous plan of his gave them all free rein to treat him worse than they had before.

So much talking. A fun day of meetings and Shilo was antsy, irritated, and jonesing to rip something apart.

Having Waylon positioned within feet of her, his pine

smell tickling her nose, was driving her hormones into a frenzy. Too bad talking to her parents about her recent sex life hadn't put a damper on them. All it had served to do was remind Shilo of how satisfying it would be to get fucked by Waylon again.

One time with him would satiate her more than an entire night with a human, that was for damn sure. Even a whole night with another shifter still left her aching and planning her next excursion, a feeling she knew she wouldn't get with Waylon.

Yet she couldn't bring herself to call one of her hookups in Ironhorse Falls and ask to come over tonight. Odd, both in that she cared about what Waylon thought after what he'd done, and that she wasn't willing to override her best intentions after a day of hearing her parents throw their weight around. That usually tickled her developing dark side, the unbonded part of her that was left without anchor and raging against authority.

But she wasn't balanced. She still had a problem and meditation wasn't going to will this internal itch away. Restless energy. A lonely shifter's worst enemy.

I'm not a fucking rogue.

Well, she might be soon. She was winning the battle momentarily, but as soon as the sun set, she needed to run. To hunt.

Her stomach turned at the thought of waking up tomorrow morning with a gut ache and a vague recollection of small animal screams and fur between her teeth.

The room emptied out, pack leaders splitting off with her parents into the hallway where they could tackle their own agendas. They ignored her for the most part as if they recognized that with two healthy parents, she wasn't taking over anytime soon.

"We still need to grab groceries." Waylon's rumble interfered with her thoughts.

"Are we going to play up our discord?" Because she was tired and the longer he was around, the harder it was to be angry at him. Defeated, maybe. Her own internal battle used too much concentration.

"It'd be a good time to test it out. It won't be hard, will it?" Waylon's teasing tone tweaked her nerves.

"Not at all," she snarled. "I think anyone who remembers you will recall your attitude."

She got up and stomped out. Hopefully, he thought she was hungry and not ready to maim something or someone.

He stayed behind her all the way to his Jeep. They might as well announce his presence in the light of day.

The drive to the grocery store was quiet. His avid gaze touched on every part of Ironhorse Falls that they passed. Five years wasn't a long time to creatures like them, but the days could be eternity. She scanned her surroundings. Nothing had changed, and that wasn't for the better. Limited shipments meant fewer home improvement supplies. But gardens flourished. Pens of chickens took over backyards and fruit trees were manicured and maintained for optimal production. They were back to growing as much of their own food as they could.

Langdon might think he was hindering Ironhorse Falls, and he was in a way. But there was strength in the old ways, resource in being self-sufficient. It made them tighter as a community. Modern didn't always equal fittest. They were creatures of the Earth, charged with protecting the land, and it would provide. How would Langdon lead if Covet were cut off from modern amenities? Would he hitch up his Hermès belt and get his Brooks Brothers loafers dirty digging in the dirt? Other than to manipulate and dominate, did he even remember what being a shifter was like?

How ironic that as she was fighting the lure of going

rogue and freeing herself from pack constraints, he was undermining her in order to control her. Wrong time of the lifespan, buddy.

Waylon parked facing out at the warehouse that was Ironhorse Grocery. She got out and shut the door with more force than she'd intended.

He walked three steps behind her the whole way into the store. The only time he got close to her was to choose an item from a shelf and carefully place it in a pile that didn't touch hers in the cart. God forbid his bacon mingle with her chopped fruit.

"Would a vegetable kill you?" *Would trying to be nice kill her?*

Just putting on a show. Her crankiness fit the situation.

He pitched his answer low. "The ones in here might. No wonder everyone grows their own."

"The trip to Freemont before this last time, I brought back as many canning jars as I could fit in the Suburban C&C lent me. I think I bought out two Walmarts' and three Targets' worth of jars. But it'll be worth it in the winter."

She puffed up with pride. Langdon Covet wasn't going to keep her people down. Surprisingly, Waylon didn't question why they hadn't confronted Langdon and physically fought against him. Waylon had enough faith in her family to know that they would make sure they had proof of his machinations before they attacked. Mother and Father hoped to throw Langdon off his game when they finally made their play. But first they had to know what the game was.

Langdon left no hard evidence, and Waylon's arrival and bold claims threw a fuzzy wrench into her parents' plans. And Shilo couldn't argue that it wasn't for the better.

The cooler she approached was filled with steaks that she wanted to load into her cart. Her inclination for red, bloody meat was stronger than ever. But she chose two four-packs and left the rest for the other residents. As if sensing her wish to help supplies stretch farther, Waylon selected the same amount and a roast.

She wouldn't even pick as much as she had, but three families from each pack had been assigned ranching duties and their herds were growing, thriving in the lush clearings prepared for them.

Food wasn't the issue. But limited movement and communication also decreased healthcare availability, access to the mating pool, and general morale. Progress was the goal and Langdon and his shifters were taking that away.

The cashier was a young girl. She eyed Waylon with appreciation, her eyes full of question, probably sensing the tension radiating between Shilo and her mate. When did she get to quit calling him her mate? Waylon, for his part, ignored the cashier and watched the store. Five people wandered in and did a double take, their shocked gazes darting from him to her. She gave each one a tight smile. Yeah, they were playing this animosity thing off well.

She paid and started to push the cart outside when Waylon growled, "Wait."

She curled her lip toward him, belatedly realizing why she shouldn't walk away from her hired bodyguard.

Finally, his items were rung up, paid for, and in the cart. She lifted her chin as they walked to the Jeep. The two of them were the stars of the show, all eyes on them. Major, one of the pack leaders, dipped his head. Relief swirled through her. Passing one person who knew about them shouldn't be any different than the rest of the colony. Was the relief for her sake, or for Waylon's? He'd been the one getting shady stares. The *what's he doing back?* looks. Not her. She could do no wrong.

Tonight she'd do a little wrong. She'd eat, stomach what she could, and at midnight she'd run.

CHAPTER 6

*S*taring at the ceiling wasn't getting him to sleep.

Waylon sighed and rolled over. The central air was going, but really, how long was it going to be before Ironhorse Falls experienced electrical outages?

Rolling to his side, he stared at the wall, getting lost in the intricate design of the wall hanging. It was a star pattern made with beads of various sizes and colors secured into a dream catcher. There was one on each wall.

Shilo had made them. He recalled her pride when she'd displayed this one to her mom, Shilene's bittersweet smile because Shilo could make fantastic wall hangings. Her gift was in crafting—and absolutely useless as a colony leader. Eventually, Shilo had stopped showing Shilene her pieces. An unimportant gift was better than no gift, but she used to talk to him late at night, afraid she'd let down her people without a mental ability that could protect them.

He'd reassured her there was a reason she could conjure the crafts her people requested. And she'd gotten a lot of orders. Ironhorse Falls had several human mates, ranging from Native American to Norwegian. The mates came here from all walks of life, often leaving their cultures behind. When they learned Shilo could help them preserve traditions long after living family had turned into ancestors, they always had an order, be it jewelry, clothing, or various crafts.

But she had doubted herself, and he imagined it contributed to the way she'd turned on him.

This line of thinking wasn't going to help him sleep. He was too restless. Shilo was in her own home, therefore she should be safe. He'd limit his run to a few-hundred-yard radius from the house. It'd have to be enough.

Not bothering to dress, he treaded to the sliding door in her kitchen and stepped outside.

His nose twitched. Blood.

He inhaled again. Rabbit blood. Was someone hunting on this land?

Shifting, he relished the transition into his wolf. Bones altering, a bite of pain that hurt so good. He was stiff. How long had it been since he'd last run?

Shaking his head, he leaned back onto his haunches to stretch, releasing tension in his torso and limbering up his legs. His wolf would blend well out here. The woods around West Creek were filled with deciduous trees. During the winter, when they lost their leaves and the ground was hidden, his rich brown fur stood out more than it would here among the evergreens. In Ironhorse Falls, the gray sprinkled through his fur aided in a natural camouflage pattern that worked better around here than West Creek. There were still plenty of cottonwoods here, but not enough to make him feel like a chocolate bar running along the stark hillside.

It was the only sign that he belonged here.

He followed his nose to the source of blood. It was like a line connected him to the fresh kill. Shilo's scent was all around, but this was her home. It should be.

A bloodied heap of fur lay at the base of a tree trunk. The

floral smell of sweet clover surrounded it. Sniffing the ground, he concentrated. The kill was recent, but he detected no one nearby.

Something about the scent. Extra musk. Was this Shilo, or a relative hunting on their land? He'd met all her kin in Iron-horse Falls but admittedly hadn't spent much time around them. A guy could take only so much disdain. It didn't matter if it was Shilene's side or Weatherly's, they all looked at him like he was grit to be picked from between their claws.

In his human form, he'd have frowned at the dead rabbit. Droplets of red splattered the tree and covered the ground. Every drop had been shaken out of the tiny creature, but all its meat was in place.

Why kill and not eat it?

That was just wrong. It wasn't how shifters worked.

A faint squeal caught his attention.

Sprinting toward the noise, he stepped lightly to keep from making a sound.

The animal scream was cut off. Dead. He pushed his speed to catch the culprit.

Sneaking around a wide tree trunk with low-hanging pine branches, he stopped.

A heartbreakingly familiar wolf was crouched over a dead mound of rabbit. Shilo's mottled brown wolf matched her hair coloring, one of the features that set them apart from regular wolves. Rich brown fur broken up by charcoal lines blended perfectly into the summery forest surrounding them. During the winter, her coat would lighten and—

What was she doing?

She growled and picked up the body. His ears picked up the crack of bones. Blood flew, and Shilo launched the animal into the air, only to catch it with a snap and repeat the process.

The...rabbit?...was already dead. There was nothing he could do for it, so he watched. What was Shilo up to?

His astonishment glued him in place when Shilo opened her jaw, dropped the rabbit, and loped off without even a small bite. The sickly sweet smell of death permeated the air.

He let out a low howl, one the occupants of the house couldn't hear.

She stopped and spun around, teeth bared, and snarled.

Whoa. There was no recognition in her gaze, just murder. He almost backed up a step.

But this was Shilo. She rarely ate in her wolf form, did so only to keep her hunting skills sharp, but she much preferred grilled veggies and a rare hunk of prime rib.

She advanced. He hadn't tried mental speak since he'd gotten back, but as mates they used to talk constantly as they ran the woods.

Shilo.

She didn't stop.

What would he do if she attacked?

She launched into the air. He skittered to the side, but she corrected and caught his flank with a paw.

Fire lanced his side.

Shilo! Stop!

Don't tell me what to do.

Her response stunned him, and she took advantage of his pause.

As she lunged for his neck, her fangs gleamed in the moonlight. He darted to the side and twisted out of reach.

What are you going to do, shake me to death like that animal?

She didn't hesitate. Had she lost her mind sometime between supper and bedtime?

She surged for him again. He couldn't run to his right. A felled tree blocked his way. He pivoted and leaped over it.

She followed, but he'd already leaped back.

I can do this all night. He couldn't. *Shilo, talk to me.*

I don't listen to you.

Well, yeah. He knew that, but there was venom in her words. A deeper meaning. *You're not acting like yourself.*

As if you'd know.

Low blow. He backed up and ran around a large, droopy pine. *You can't chase me all night.*

I said don't tell me what to do.

She ducked under the boughs and caught him midrun. He tumbled to the side, claws and teeth ripping at his pelt. *Fucking ow. Stop it, Shilo.*

You're not the boss of me!

What are we, five?

You're. Nothing.

Enough about the old Shilo. Where was the female he'd spent the last two days with? She wasn't going to stop. Earlier yesterday, she'd acted less hostile when she'd had the grounds to berate him. What was going on with her?

He writhed and twisted, moving any which way he could to keep her from gaining a hold on him.

A weathered log lurked at the corner of his vision, and with a grunt, he shifted to his human form, the burn of her claws crisper as they slipped from his changing form. He grabbed her with both hands and flung her headfirst into the log.

The crack went straight to his stomach. As she fell limp to the ground, he could've hurled. but it'd been the only way to stop her.

His sides heaved. He looked around. The area surrounding him had fallen silent. Blood trickled down his body from the cuts and gashes her claws and teeth had left behind. But he'd heal. And so would she.

He didn't have time to worry about the carcasses. Getting

Shilo inside and coaxing her to shift back to her human form before she went batshit again was his priority.

Hefting her to his shoulder, he tried not to groan at the pain coursing through his body. He cradled her like the precious cargo she was and trotted to the door he'd come out of. Once he was inside, he took a full breath. Climbing the stairs and going straight to her bed, he had a million questions. Laying her down on her hand-quilted comforter, he cursed himself. She was bloody and a piece of rabbit intestine was staining the quilt. But the worry was swept away by questions.

Was this the first time it'd happened? Did she always hunt like this? Had she just been hungry?

She'd eaten a good supper.

Or had she?

They'd grilled. Well, he'd grilled after she'd prepared the food for him. That way they could be in separate areas. Then she'd taken her food to the porch and he'd eaten at the table. But she must not have had leftovers; otherwise she would've gobbled up the fresh rabbit meat. Only fucking rogues left kill to rot.

His breath froze. He gazed down at the limp form of his fated mate. They were mates, but they hadn't bonded their souls.

Shifters eventually went crazy if they didn't bond. But they could live for centuries without finding their mate.

But some went rogue before that happened.

He'd only been gone five years.

But some went rogue earlier than others. There was no explanation. Mating and madness were very individual experiences.

Fuck, he'd only been gone five years. And yeah, he'd been feeling restless lately, but not homicidal. Not kill-baby-bunnies murderous.

His gaze brushed over her rich brown coat. It shouldn't be possible. She was the most centered shifter he knew.

The wolf twitched and morphed into a beautifully naked female. She groaned and rolled to the side, out cold. He tucked her under the blanket and winced at the red stains on the covers. He'd have to look up how to get blood out of cherished material.

Slumping, he buried his head in his hands. Sweet Mother, what had he done? All those years ago, he'd walked out, thinking he was leaving her to the life she wanted, to the life she thought she deserved. But she'd attacked him tonight. Him. Her mate. All because he'd left her and hadn't thought twice about the consequences.

He'd condemned her.

His mate was going rogue.

~

THE POUNDING in her head woke her.

Why does my head hurt so badly?

She rolled over and groaned.

A male's scent wafted over her. She wasn't alone.

Who'd she…?

Waylon. Had they— Had she—

She pried her eyes open and with her next breath, she smelled scared animal and dead animal.

She'd gone out hunting. No, that wasn't the right word. She'd gone out killing.

Her gaze focused on a somber male sitting on the changing stool she kept in her closet.

His elbows rested on his knees and his hands were clasped together. His oak-bark brown eyes were on her.

He knew.

She didn't know how he knew, she couldn't remember—

Images assaulted her.

Nope. She recalled it all.

Closing her eyes and rolling onto her back, she couldn't think of anything to say but "You know."

"Figured it out." He sounded like he'd gargled with gravel this morning.

"Gonna tell anyone?"

"Dunno." The rustling of clothes signaled his rising. His soft footsteps on her hardwood quieted when he stepped on the rag rug on the other side of her bed. The bed sank under his weight. "When did you start having problems?"

She laughed bitterly. "Do you know how long I waited to sleep with someone after you left?" Did he know how long she'd waited for him to come back? "Then the urges hit. A little desire here, some horniness there. I hadn't heard a word from you and finally, I just couldn't help it."

His breath heaved out and the bed moved again as he lay down next to her. She was under the quilt and he was over it. Safe enough.

"I threw up after the first time with someone else, you know." Had he? Would that make her feel better? Or sadder? "But I couldn't stop. The needs. Then...the anger followed. It's my job to take orders from my parents and carry out their wishes. Suddenly, it was like I was a teenager again, getting resentful when they'd pass along instructions. Moody. I didn't want to listen to anyone. And the sex got rougher."

"Your moods?"

Another humorless chuckle escaped her. "Would you believe yesterday was better than most days? I can hide it though. I've been hiding it. I don't know how much longer I can keep it up."

"What made yesterday better?"

Her mouth flattened. "I assumed it was from the night

before, but it doesn't make sense. He wasn't memorable enough to remember."

Several emotions passed through his eyes. Displeasure. Heartbreak. Smugness. Then he gave a humorless snort. "Not-memorable-enough encounters about describes my last couple of years."

"Yeah." She stared at the ceiling. Never would she have thought she'd be in her bed with Waylon talking about their lackluster sex life with other people. "Are you going to tell my parents?"

"Why haven't *you* told them?"

Good question. It wouldn't be an easy conversation. But why hadn't she told them? Did she have a drive to do it all alone? It's not as if she hadn't thought of their reaction.

"Several reasons, I guess, but I kept thinking that maybe I'd get better." And that she might find someone to bond to stave off the madness.

"No, I won't tell them."

She ignored the pounding in her head to look at him. He was staring at the ceiling like she'd been doing. "Why?" Was it his history with her family?

"They have Langdon to worry about, and the fewer people who know, the less chance the information will get back to the Covet pack."

She let out a gusty breath and returned her stare to the ceiling. Watching his profile in such a familiar spot ignited an ache in her chest she'd thought she'd recovered from. "All right. There's not much to do today."

"Then rest." Waylon rolled up. "Meditate. Whatever keeps you from wanting to slaughter forest creatures."

She winced and sat up much slower than he did. "I have to go take care of my mess."

"Already done. I'll be downstairs when you get up." Waylon strode out of her room.

He was taking care of her. All he'd been hired for was extra security, another obstacle for Covet to keep from orchestrating a way to trap her in their colony. But Waylon was taking care of her.

She lay in her bed for several more minutes, relishing the lack of restlessness roiling under her skin. Calm. A rare feeling for her these days.

But it wouldn't last long. It never did anymore.

CHAPTER 7

A whole day had passed and Shilo had managed to function like a normal person both inside and out. Right now she was in bed, having woken from a night of tossing and turning.

Yesterday, after she'd cleaned up and eaten, she'd spent most of her day at home in her crafting room. Waylon had hung around but hadn't been in the way. So many times, she'd wanted to chat but stopped herself. They weren't acrimonious, but they weren't friends either. The complication of being destined mates who hadn't worked out, then having to pal around while one or both moved on with their lives, was too difficult.

How did he do it? Could she have gone to that bar he worked at and stood against the wall while he went about his life?

For the evening, she'd retreated to her craft room. It had been a guest bedroom next to hers, but she didn't have guests over. The act of threading beads should've been relaxing, but the itchiness was growing. Being alone made it worse, like the madness sensed she was supposed to be with someone and so it spurred her to find anyone.

Would Waylon look the other way if she went killing tonight?

Her stomach turned. How many more mornings of being sick to her stomach and brimming with regret over her treatment of nature could she handle? It went against her shifter self.

Mother had survived centuries without a mate. Which would disappoint her more? That Shilo couldn't make it more than a few years without Waylon, or that she wasted bunnies to hide her secret?

Why couldn't Shilo live without a mate while surrounded by her friends, family, and pack?

It wasn't fair.

She caught herself sneering at the ceiling.

It was almost eight a.m. and she had to get moving. They had a long drive to Freemont for the meeting with Langdon. Waylon was anticipating being stopped in Passage Lake. He wanted to leave with plenty of time to spare.

She went through her routine and after spacing out in the shower for a few minutes, she was done and made her way downstairs.

She sniffed. Waylon's scent was permeating her home once again. She should be upset. It'd taken patience and effort to wipe his presence out before. But the closer she got to food and him, the more her tension uncoiled, the tightness dissipating—not going away, but retreating, weakening.

The savory smell of sausage in the air must be his doing. Her stomach rumbled. Turning into the kitchen, her fangs dropped. Waylon's back was to her. He wore a clean shirt, but it was exactly like the others he wore. Hanes tee in white, black, or blue. Today's was black, his security outfit. That boxing had done his body good. The wide set of his shoulders tapered into his waist but was offset by his thick thighs. A perfectly proportioned specimen of a male.

His longish hair was the same as it'd always been, like when she'd first seen him prowling around town, his face full of suspicion over what other shifters would say or do. He didn't know it, but he'd inspired many a female shifter's naughty dreams, the bad boy all of them wanted a shot at but who none of them wanted to stick around.

Shilo had. She'd been sexually attracted to him from the get-go, but it was his face. Those mysterious, dark eyes that saw everything, and that lush, full mouth that commented on nothing. She almost smiled. How that trait had changed.

His lower lip was fuller than his top, and his nose was just a little crooked. His face was longer than it was square, but his chiseled chin kept him from looking gangly. He was strong. Inside and out.

Just not strong enough to stick around.

She slumped into a chair and snagged a link of deer sausage. Munching on it, she shifted in her seat. Sweet Mother, couldn't she go more than two days without sex before the urges hit?

When Waylon was around? No.

"The Jeep is ready," Waylon said. His back muscles flexed as he dumped a pile of eggs from the pan to the plate. She could groan. He'd scrambled eggs in the sausage grease and it was fucking amazing. "I just have to gas up before we leave town."

"'Kay." Shoving more food into her mouth so she didn't have to talk, she hunched over her plate.

The platter with the eggs was slid in front of her. She couldn't look at him without the burn blooming in her belly.

Using the excuse of refilling her plate to hide the movement, she ground her ass into the chair.

Waylon dropped his fork and sat back. "We can't go rolling through Covet with you smelling so ripe."

"I showered," she growled.

"Ripe in a way that makes all of us males want to sink our teeth into you."

A flush crept up her cheeks. "I can't help it." She stabbed another sausage link.

Waylon's chair scraped along the floor as he pushed it back. Picking up his plate and fork, he left the kitchen and went out the sliding door.

She chewed but the meat could've been dust. This was going to be a long trip.

MEASURED BREATHING for over two and a half hours wore him down like a thirty-mile run through rolling hills loaded with trees.

Waylon sucked in a breath, wishing he could warp his nose and block out Shilo's heady scent. She was more turned on than he'd ever seen her.

But from the prim way she sat in the passenger seat, with her shiny black fuck-me shoes and burgundy pantsuit, no one could tell. Her sleek hair was secured in a—what had she called it?—a French twist.

He wore black jeans, a black shirt, and black boots, and he'd been calculating the fastest ways to strip her down for the last 155 minutes.

Passage Lake was approaching. His Jeep was working fine and they had plenty of time before they had to meet Langdon in the back room of a trendy restaurant. The owner was a "friend." A friend that was probably male and willing to sleep with Shilo.

Was that Langdon's kink?

Waylon passed by the gas station in Passage Lake that Langdon had stopped them at. The two gas stations in town acted like guard posts. Paulie manned the station on the other end of town. Did Langdon take post in this one? Waylon couldn't see anyone, but something was sending shivers up and down his spine.

"We're being watched," he said.

"Of course," Shilo replied. She gazed out the window like the damn princess she was, her ski-jump nose in the air and her chin lifted.

Idling through town brought no activity. Waylon tensed as Paulie's place approached. Two cars were at the gas pumps, but no one was walking between them and the convenience store. One of the big service doors was open, but again, no movement from inside.

They were almost past when the hair on the back of Waylon's neck stood up.

"Wait for it." He gripped the wheel and looked around. While he should be ecstatic that he had more confirmation of an ability, the situation robbed his elation.

A pop resonated through the night, followed by a *flap, flap, flap*.

"They blew a tire." He pulled over on the side of the road. "Dammit."

Waylon dug out a tire change kit and rolled the spare next to the blown tire that was inconveniently located on the driver's side where his ass would hang out in traffic. A shadow caught his eye and the smell of burning oil and exhaust hit his nose. Paulie stood in the darkness of the garage.

Waylon straightened and turned around, calling to Paulie, "Wanna do me a favor and not blow another tire?"

The corner of Paulie's mouth went up to reveal a long fang.

Waylon slid his measured stare away to get to work.

A door slammed. He jerked his head up. Heels ground into the pavement as Shilo strode across the highway.

Where the fuck— He glanced over his shoulder.

Her hips had an extra swing, her leggy walk mesmerizing. Paulie was hooked.

"Paulie," Shilo purred, the sound traveling straight to Waylon's cock.

"Ms. Ironhorse." The lust in Paulie's voice spurred Waylon on.

Using every advantage of his species, he changed the tire in minutes, straining to hear Shilo and Paulie. But as he tossed his tools into the backseat, Shilo's heels clicked back toward him.

She ignored him and climbed in.

Nothing but a dutiful bodyguard.

He got in and slammed the door. As he twisted to glare at her, his gaze dipped down to where the top two buttons of her pink blouse were strategically undone. "What'd you two talk about?"

"Idle small talk. I wanted to make him so damn uncomfortable he gets his dick caught in the zipper of his overalls."

He paused, putting his vehicle in drive. "You went over there just to shower your pheromones all over him and leave?"

"I shouldn't be the only one uncomfortable."

"You're not. Believe me."

CHAPTER 8

*W*aylon was Shilo's shadow. The best part of the day had been enjoying Langdon's reaction to seeing him with Shilo. The male's eye had twitched, his lips went flat, and the hard look he gave Waylon had bordered on murderous.

Yeah, the guy was up to something.

If that hadn't been his first clue, the room full of virile male specimens would be his next. Only one other female shifter mingled in the crowd and she resembled Langdon enough to be confidently labeled a relative. The other male shifter in the room also had the Covet look and wasn't eying Shilo like he was imagining the number of sexual positions he could pretzel her into.

Shilo kept her hands folded in front of her, doing a half bow when Langdon introduced her to individuals. Did she come here smelling like sin on heels every time?

Waylon concentrated on the spicy aromas of the Chinese fare served at the establishment instead of her, but that back-fired. His stomach threatened to rumble but he tightened his abs to keep it from happening. Bodyguards don't stand watch, craving kung pao chicken.

The human men in the room were enraptured by her. Her regal features, her taller-than-average stature, and those two fucking buttons revealing bronzed, creamy flesh weren't lost on humans. Her suit jacket tucked in at her trim waist and flared over her ample hips. The ensemble didn't make her look like a waif, but enhanced the strength and power of her body. Add in her sexual vibes and the men might as well hang their tongues out.

Each time one looked Waylon's way, they glanced away again within a second.

The occupants of the room were seated around a long table. Serving staff came and went from a side entrance with trays of water, egg drop soup, and egg rolls. As negotiations progressed, Waylon learned more than he wanted to about laying cable, access multipliers, and last-mile connectivity. Shilo was charming and savvy, and by the time the main course arrived, the contractors had promised the fastest internet at the best prices by the fall. That they were going to dig hundreds of miles of line in a few months, Waylon wanted to call bullshit. Unfortunately, there weren't other options for Shilo. These people had worked with Langdon, and another company would have to start from Freemont and cover the entire distance, bringing the concern back to the original problem: How would they get around the Covet pack?

Everyone turned to their food and instead of ignoring him like most powerful men would do with bodyguards, Langdon pinned him with a bright amber stare. "Waylon, I hear you're from Ironhorse Falls originally."

"Yep." Waylon was standing behind Shilo, but the stiffening of her shoulders was visible.

Langdon's shrewd gaze stayed on him, his plate of

noodles steaming across his features, untouched. "I was born and raised in Passage Lake and have worked closely with Ironhorse Falls for years. I don't recall you. What's your last name?"

"Wolf."

Langdon's mouth flattened. The male showed his displeasure easily. Had he thought Waylon was messing with him? Wolf was more than an ironic last name, it was intentional. Uncle Wolf had never let on that it wasn't his real last name, but Waylon had assumed it wasn't. The whole colony had, too, but since they wanted little to do with the wacky hermit who lived in the woods and the wild child he'd adopted, no one had pressed the issue.

Langdon switched his attention to Shilo. "You two grew up together. Is that how he became your…escort?"

Shilo rolled lo mien onto her fork. "Yes. He's my ex." She shoved the food into her mouth and chewed like nothing was wrong.

Lips in a hard line. Two issues with Langdon. He hated not having the upper hand when it came to information, and he didn't like it not being freely shared. Which one was it in this case? Waylon had been around two days, but Langdon wasn't letting on what had filtered down to him.

"How magnanimous of him." Langdon's grip on his chopsticks was tight enough to snap them.

"Mmm." Shilo's patronizing response was lost as she worked on her food. *Way to go, princess. Make him wonder.*

Waylon watched him. Yes, Langdon must have heard he and Shilo were mates and the male was not happy to have the tidbit confirmed. Waylon needed to find out what Langdon had planned for Shilo that a mate hanging around would interfere with.

"Is Shilo what brought you back to Ironhorse Falls, or are you there to stay?" Langdon still hadn't touched his food despite his hand clutching the chopsticks hovering over his plate.

Waylon lifted a shoulder. "We'll see."

The answer didn't please the shifter. "Indeed, we shall."

The internet contractor on Shilo's right asked her about Ironhorse Falls' amenities and the conversation turned. Waylon kept his post and tried to forget his hunger. He surreptitiously studied all the men in the room. A couple were married, and while they seemed enamored with Shilo, their intentions were nothing more than simple male awareness. The obviously single men though... A younger internet contractor who had started the current conversation, Tim, was leaning closer, his eyes twinkling, his human scent full of lust. Another man in his mid-thirties across the table had a calculating gleam in his gray eyes as he followed the lively conversation, never taking his gaze off Shilo.

Had Langdon promised one of them that Shilo would go to bed with him? Both of them? What was Langdon's game?

The epiphany hit Waylon. Langdon was plying Shilo with human sex partners who couldn't claim her and who she wouldn't fall in love with or mate. The latter might be a worry, but that was eliminated since it wasn't a secret her mate had left.

Was the Covet shifter going to make a play for Shilo himself? Try to mate her with one of his own pack? Or keep her single and therefore presumably weaker?

Langdon was up to something.

Shilo's tinkling laugh made Waylon's fangs throb. That was her flirty laugh. It'd haunted his dreams for the last five years.

Now the man's hand rested on the back of her chair and she'd turned, crossing one long leg over the other to chat with him. Another laugh and she lightly touched the contractor's shoulder.

Waylon's tunnel stare nearly blocked out Langdon's smug smile. The shifter was sly enough not to aim it at Waylon, but it was there. Langdon pushed away from the table. It must've been the signal to end dinner. The married guys each checked their watches and commented about kids' practices and running an errand for the wife. The human woman in the group huddled with Langdon for a few moments before leaving.

Shilo was absorbed in the discussion with Tim. The other gawker was checking his phone and would likely jet soon. The only others that remained were the two Covet shifters.

Shilo's throaty laugh was another kick in the groin. "I'll meet you at the bar. Excuse me."

Blood rushed between Waylon's ears. She would what?

She slipped out of her chair and went for the door without looking at Waylon. He caught her tight expression. Her smile had faded and the lines at her eyes strained like they were holding back floodwaters.

He started after her.

Langdon's faux-cultured voice carried above the others. "Surely she can use the restroom on her own?"

Since Waylon didn't answer to the shifter, he walked out.

The echo of heels clicked down the tiled floor. Murals of women working on the shoreline decorated the walls on either side. The main part of the establishment was brightly lit, but the hallways were dim.

"Shilo," he hissed. Her hearing would be enough he didn't have to shout.

Her steps faltered, then sped up.

He picked up his pace and turned the corner as she disappeared into the ladies room. Reaching the door before she locked it, he shouldered his way inside and let the door close behind him. Catching her eye, he locked the door.

Her soft brown irises were a swirl of anger and panic.

Was she afraid he'd make a scene and ruin it for her contractor?

"What the fuck, Shilo?" He could barely keep from shouting, so he whisper-yelled. "'Meet you at the bar'? Do you think I'm going to drive you to his house and stand outside the bedroom door while you're fucking?" He shoved a hand through his hair. It was either that or hit a wall. She was picking a guy up in front of him? The separation between them had never been more apparent.

Her nostrils flared and she poked a finger into the meaty part of his shoulder so hard he staggered back.

"What else am I supposed to do?" Her whisper was harsh and ragged. "I feel like I can rip this restaurant apart brick by brick." He didn't mention the building was made of lumber. "It was all I could do not to throw the food against the wall and shatter the plates. All the 'You'll have to have this ready by the time we trench' and 'You'll need to clear this with the mayor.' I'm going crazy!" She stepped away, and he instantly missed the heat of her body.

Spinning so her back was to him, she dropped her forehead into one hand, the other propped on her hip.

"There are only so many options for a rogue and I'm running out of them."

His fury drained away. She didn't want to sleep with that man, but she thought there was no other option.

Grasping her elbow, he tugged her back toward him. "I have an idea."

SHILO'S back was against the wall and Waylon's strong body lined up with hers. The hard length of him pressed into her and it was better than she remembered. She didn't have to argue because the only thought going through her mind and body was *At last*.

"I can give you relief." Hot breath fanned over her face, sending shivers down her neck. "You don't need him."

"This…" *Can't happen*. Her chest was heaving. His head was tilted over her, his body primed to do a job it did excellently. She just had to get the rest of the sentence out. Instead, she tugged his head down and kissed him.

He kissed her back, his erection grinding into her belly. She anchored herself on his shoulders and widened her stance. Her core needed that hardness rubbed against it.

Why the hell had she worn pants today?

He flicked open the hook and eye clasp on her slacks and shoved his hand down them. Hot fingers covered her sex, seeking her clit.

Yesss.

She rolled her hips into him and plundered his mouth with her tongue. Heat bloomed between them as her body opened for his touch.

As soon as his fingers found her supercharged nub, she bowed against the door, ripping her mouth off him. "Yes!"

He crashed his lips back onto hers. Oh, right. Discretion.

Rocking her hips, she planted one heel against the door and supported her weight with her other leg and Waylon's body. His expert touch and her raging hormones drove her toward her peak within a minute without penetration.

She tried to open her mouth to call out as her orgasm hit, but he swallowed her cry. Helpless against the waves of pleasure and his immovable form, she shook her release.

Sensing she was done, he removed his hand, released her mouth. Her head hit the door as her breathing caught up with her oxygen needs.

Opening her eyes, she smiled, her body going molten

from head to toe. "I liked the appetizer." She reached for his waistband.

He jerked away, backing up two steps. Any more and he'd fall onto the toilet. The stormy expression on his face registered.

"No." His jaw was tight, his eyes flashing.

"What's your problem?" Her hackles were rising and her defenses slammed back up. He'd just gotten her off and now he was acting like he couldn't stand to touch her, that she'd done something wrong. *He'd* stuck *his* hand down her pants.

"My problem," he said in a low, hard tone that shouldn't turn her on so much, "is that I'm not going to be the one to blame when your aggression dies down and you realize that we fucked."

He stepped to the side and then spun back the other way. There wasn't enough room to pace in the bathroom. She sank against the cool wood of the door to wait for him to finish.

She wouldn't have blamed him for having sex with her. But…the spinning thoughts in her mind were slowing down, enough to admit she might have been horrified she'd jumped Waylon as soon as her guard was down.

"So this is what you're gonna do, *princess*." He stabbed a finger toward the door. "You're going to go to the bar and meet with *that guy*." His lip curled to reveal a fang. "And you're going to decide if you want to burn your rage on others or let me service you until we figure out how else we can help you. But I want this to be *your* decision, Shilo. No one is going to tell you what to do."

She opened her mouth, then closed it again. He was ordering her around and she should be pissed, her rage should be increasing, her inner wolf howling.

He was right. Sex with him had the potential to ruin her. What if he walked again? With or without warning, if she couldn't keep her emotions out of it, he could destroy her. She'd go from the edge of disobedience straight over the line into insanity.

Worrying about what Waylon thought and how it might hurt him if she slept with someone else was a moot point. None of her concern. He was the reason she was bordering on madness.

But right now, she was…calm. Rational. As close to her old self as she'd been for a while. This was the best moment to decide how she was going to carry out her future.

CHAPTER 9

*S*hilo threw her head back as she sank down on the hard length. Her body was greedy and ready. There was no foreplay, no waiting. This was hard, fast fucking in the backseat.

She'd sat in the bar, flirting with Tim, taking her time to make her decision as Langdon's cousin Oscar hit on a woman at the end of the bar. He'd been spying on her, so she'd flirted with Tim harder.

The release was necessary, there was no question about that. She just had to choose who. Other girls might relish the decision, but not her. She hated being at the mercy of these urges, skipping the getting-to-know-you phase and totally blowing off the can-I-see-you-again step. She missed cuddling, mourned the laughter and the heart-to-hearts, and dreamed of being able to act silly with a male she trusted.

Squeezing her eyes shut, she rocked back to keep her head from hitting the roof. She would've laughed but she was riding her partner too hard. He was happy to let her do all the work while he flicked her nipples through her still-buttoned shirt. They'd skipped foreplay. She'd made her decision when the clock had hit eleven, and she'd dragged him out of the bar to fuck in his ride.

She tipped her head to the side to keep from whacking into the roof. Muscle memory. Is that what they called it? She knew exactly how to arch and stretch to keep from getting stuck between the front seats and giving herself a concussion while she threw her head around.

"Fuck, Shilo," Waylon grunted, pumping in and out of her with the inch of leeway she gave him.

Her knees scraped against the upholstery of the Jeep. The poor slacks she'd worn were getting pummeled underneath Waylon's boots, and Shilo thought she'd heard a seam on the shoulder of her jacket rip, but she didn't care.

Waylon was inside her once again.

He hadn't said more than "it's unlocked" once she'd told him it was time to go. She'd handed Tim her number—not her *real* number—and made sure Oscar saw before she left. But Oscar had been too busy chatting with the blonde next to him while the young bartender glowered at them. Had the bartender been after the blonde or Oscar?

Shilo twisted enough to lean forward over him, her ass grinding into Waylon's thighs. He might've come once already, but he hadn't slowed and she'd paid attention only to her own needs.

"Suck on them." She ripped open her shirt and thrust her chest in his face the extra half inch they had to spare.

He clamped his teeth around a nipple through her lacy bra. Why the fuck had she worn a bra in the first place? It was piss-poor armor and she'd planned to get naked tonight anyway.

Her second orgasm for the night slammed into her. It brought enough clarity to ponder whether the parking lot had surveillance cameras. What would they see? A black Jeep rocking at the edge of the light a weak street lamp threw off?

Waylon wouldn't have let this happen where perverts could be voyeurs.

Another wave of need washed over her. And his T-shirt was in the way.

She bunched the material in her fists and ripped it off. He did nothing but grunt and bite down harder on her breast.

"More," she said. Being demanding, verbalizing what she wanted, had never been a part of her relationship with Waylon. He'd always known what she needed. But she'd changed. This was new territory.

She raked down his sides with her nails and rode him faster than she had before.

It wasn't enough. Grabbing his hand off her waist, she stuffed it between them. He had to adjust to keep tonguing her peaked nipple and find her wet sex. Her bouncing wasn't helping things.

With a frustrated cry, she wrenched herself off him. "It's not enough."

He flipped her next to him, keeping her on her knees and wedged himself behind her. Why hadn't they rented a room? She could've waited that long.

He shoved inside of her from behind, and she rejoiced. No, she couldn't have waited.

Sweat beaded along her forehead, and most of her hair had fallen out of its clip. The windows of the Jeep were steaming. She kept her hand off the glass to keep some do-gooder from checking on her and interrupting this for one millisecond.

This was too good to stop.

He thrust in and out, hard enough to bump her head against the backdoor panel, but it gave him a little extra room to circle her clit with this finger while keeping her open to maximum penetration.

This would do.

She wrapped an arm around the headrest and nearly ripped it off as the climax hit. Waylon groaned and swelled even thicker as his hot release spilled inside of her.

Oh yes. This is what she'd been missing. A male, not a man. A guy who could sustain multiple orgasms without resting in between. A guy whose length and thickness put her past human partners to shame. A guy who could give it to her just like she needed it.

He withdrew and spun her again, spreading her legs until one hung over the backseat into the cargo area and the other splayed across the console in the front. She was wide open and glistening from all the sex they'd had in just a few short minutes.

Shifting backward as much as he could, he pushed his way inside. They fucked like this for another release, then anther, until she was nearly howling with her euphoria. He dominated her. Intent, ruthless, he gave her orgasm after orgasm until she went limp. Only then did he collapse over her.

"You didn't come," she murmured, her eyes barely staying open.

"Hell yeah, I did. Just not that last time. 'Sokay." His sides were heaving and his head rested on her chest. He was probably mooning whoever or whatever was outside the back window, but they were too boneless to move.

"Yeah," she breathed. "It was okay."

He lifted his head to scowl at her.

She chuckled, surprised she had the energy for it.

He was still inside of her. His twitches resonated through her fatigue. She could totally go again, but it'd be softer, more passionate. The serious threat of a more-than-physical feeling being involved was getting higher the longer they remained like this.

She moved to sit up. He pulled out, still hard. She averted

her eyes. Seeing his erect glory still wet from being inside of her wouldn't help her emotions.

While she located her slacks and straightened them out, he wrestled his jeans up and tugged at the ends of his shirt. He pulled it off and again; she couldn't look. There wasn't enough beer on the planet to give Waylon's chiseled body a beer gut. She didn't have to look to know he was as magnificent as he'd always been.

He waited until she'd pulled her pants on before opening the door. The fresh, cool night air was a welcome relief. Strands of her hair were plastered against her face and down her neck. Buttons were missing from her top. She secured her one suit jacket button instead before getting out.

Waylon opened the console and dug out a wrinkled white tee. He tugged it on and slid into the driver's seat.

A scan of the parking lot showed a car much like what the members of the Covet pack preferred still parked by the building. Good. Oscar hadn't come outside. He might think she'd hooked up with Tim somewhere else, buying them time before Langdon figured out exactly how he was guarding her.

She got into the passenger seat, brushed her hair behind her ear, and clicked her seat belt on. "Oscar is still here. His twin, Brynley, left before…" The most excellent bathroom encounter. "We can get a hotel. I have cash in case Langdon's demented enough to trace my card."

"We're going back to Ironhorse Falls tonight." Waylon turned the key.

"But it's almost midnight."

"And he'll be expecting you to stay over. He might have anticipated this." Waylon waved to the backseat. "But he'll assume you're staying in Freemont whether you're with me or…Tim." The predatory reflection hit his pupils as he said the human's name.

"But I have supplies to pick up." Supplies she'd had no intention of getting just because the list had been handed to her with strict instructions not to forget. She needed to capitalize on the urge to do what she was supposed to.

"Then we'll hit a twenty-four-hour box store and head out. Change the routine on him, Shilo."

"Can you drive all night?"

He shrugged. "We can take turns. But if we get our shopping done and roll through Passage Lake when all the shifters have done their nightly runs and bedded down for the night, we can see what they're like unprepared."

"I like that idea. Let's go."

WAYLON'S HANDS were still shaking as he loaded the last crate of canning jars. He'd laid down the backseat and used every inch he and Shilo weren't sitting in to store their materials. Canning jars, salt, sugar, and vinegar took up over half. Then there were emergency rations like packets of tuna and chicken and as many first aid supplies as they could handle, which included more salt. Waylon wouldn't put it past Langdon to give Ironhorse Falls members a severe case of silver poisoning.

Loading his vehicle at least took his mind off what he'd done with Shilo. He'd run a gamut of emotion tonight, from the euphoria of the bathroom incident to the sinking pit in his stomach as he'd sat a couple barstools down from her and Tim. And he'd been certain she'd go home with Tim. The feeling was enough to unsettle him for years.

Her wild abandon… He'd never seen her like that. Sure, they'd been energetic before, but this had been raw. Primal.

Then once she'd relaxed even slightly and they'd stopped, she was back to prim and proper. His princess. In the store, she'd had her list and checked it twice and sent him off to grab items that were close by. In and out in forty-five minutes, cash paid.

Shilo walked their second cart back to the cart rack, her heels echoing across the nearly empty lot. The few people that were shopping had barely spared Shilo a second look in her shiny heels and rumpled business wear. She'd freed her hair, swept it back up in a self-contained messy bun, and she'd strutted around Walmart like the royalty she was.

"Want me to drive?" she asked.

"Nah. You rest. Maybe after Covet." He needed to grip something to keep his hands steady. How easily he'd slipped back into mate mindset. Four times on the way to the store, he'd stopped himself from reaching over to stroke her thigh and smile at her and think how damn lucky he was a girl like her had chosen a guy like him.

But she hadn't, and he had to keep telling himself that. Fate had, and in the end, she'd chosen her parents.

On the road, Shilo settled in, but she didn't go to sleep. She waited until they got out of town before she spoke. "What'd you do the last five years?"

He stared out the windshield. Was there anything he shouldn't tell her? Or should he be brutally honest about how bad it'd been?

"I drove aimlessly for weeks, doing odd jobs for cash. Then I decided to get legit papers so I could get a job among the humans, and that brought me to my current pack leader. Christian and his mate are the leaders of misfits like me, shifters who don't fit in anywhere but need a pack to keep from going rogue." He gave her a sidelong look.

But she didn't even flinch. "Makes sense."

"You don't look rogue," he blurted.

She arched a dark brow. "What's a rogue supposed to look like?"

"Unbathed. Ratty. Broke as hell because they don't have the support of a pack."

"That sounds more like a shifter who's gone feral. I'm not rogue yet."

"The rabbits?"

"I didn't say I wasn't on the edge."

If other pack members caught her in the woods as mindless and aggressive as the night he'd found her, she would've been detained until the pack decided how to deal with her. Which would only incite a borderline-rogue shifter.

"Anyway, what else did you do?" Change of subject. Okay, he'd go with it for now, but they'd have to circle back soon.

"Not much. I got a job as a bartender not long after meeting Christian and that's what I did." Poured drinks and fucked. "What about you?"

"My role as ambassador ramped up. I don't know if it was necessary or to keep me busy. You were gone. Charlie and Cass moved not long after and I was…listless. Useless."

"You're never useless."

Her smile was small. "Beadwork doesn't advance the colony. I get a lot of work for the annual powwow, but other than that, we don't really need it anymore."

"It's better than only being to tell when someone else is using an ability. That's shaping up to be mine." Maybe it'd be useful, but not more than killing an engine cold. "What you offer is not a tangible need, but your people need to remember their past." Even with their long lives, their culture was getting lost in the hurry to modernize. Their human relations had long passed, taking their knowledge with them.

"My people need more from me than a traditional jingle dress."

"It's your gift for a reason."

"And you were my mate for a reason. Look how that worked out."

Ouch. Her retort had been quick, without much thought. Did that make it more honest?

"We worked well together," he said. "In the end, it wasn't us working together. It was you and your parents."

"What did you expect me to do?" she snapped. "They're the colony leaders. I'm the next colony leader. Am I supposed to shun their opinion and advice? We could've still worked at it, but you didn't even try. You weren't willing to give them time—to give *me* time. You left."

"Was I supposed to stay and be your pool boy?" He let out a disgusted grunt. "This isn't getting us anywhere. Look, I'll service your needs until this Covet shit is done or you take a mate, whichever comes first."

Had he just said that? His stomach twisted. Shilo take another mate. He'd had a hard enough time watching her flirt in the bar. His temples had pounded and each minute, he'd come up with a new and eventful way to kill the innocent and oblivious dude.

"Fine. I don't really have a choice." She stared out the passenger window. The moon was high, the only other source of illumination besides his headlights. The yellow dash lights chased shadows away from the high points of her face, leaving her expression haunted.

"You always have a choice with me. I get the rogue thing, but being with me isn't an all-or-nothing deal."

"A bodyguard with benefits?" she asked. "Do you think we can do that?"

"It's part of protecting you. And let's be honest—we're not going to be mellow standing aside while one of us goes off and fucks someone else."

The set of her jaw was clear in the dashboard glow. "What do we tell people?"

"We're going to smell like each other anyway. Let them assume what they want."

"You never marked me."

No, he hadn't. So many times he'd hovered over her neck in the throes of passion, but he'd never committed. An instinct that sensed she hadn't fully accepted him? But then she'd never offered her neck. "You didn't seem ready."

He expected a rebuttal, but she stared straight ahead.

He changed the subject. "What are your plans for the next week?"

"More like the next month. I'm behind on orders for two traditional dresses. Can you believe it? I've made dresses for these girls since they were old enough to jump and now they've ordered the full-grown outfits they'll wear for years. Decades even. I feel old."

He smiled. Back in safe territory, they talked about her orders and how long she planned to work on them. There was also a powwow planning committee meeting, but Shilo didn't expect any drama. The annual powwow had been running for decades, and the major details had been ironed out long ago.

"It's a quiet week," she murmured. "We wait and see if Langdon lives up to his promises. The contractor that'll dig the line is supposed to contact Mother later next week."

All Waylon had to do, beyond looking after Shilo, was get a message to his employers. All he had to say was that the case was stable and handled. Any more and they risked Langdon intercepting it and taking advantage of the info.

Waylon looked forward to the next few weeks. If all went according to plan, it would be blessedly drama-free.

CHAPTER 10

The sun's rays snuck through a crack in her drapes and slapped a band of blinding light across her face. Shilo blinked awake and rolled over. She reached her arm out as she opened her eyes, knowing no one was on the other side of her bed. Waylon had serviced her and gone back to his room. It was their routine.

After they'd returned from Freemont three weeks ago, she'd waited until the urge to charge out to the sidewalk, yank a male off the concrete, and drag him back home, cave-girl style was too strong to ignore. Waylon had either sensed her increasing desire or noted her short, cranky answers and the way she stomped around the upper level as she attached beads to a garment.

When a two-quart canister of multicolored beads had hit the floor and she'd shouted every swear word she knew and a few she'd made up, he'd charged in and taken her against the wall. Then her craft table, knocking over another jar in the process that she suddenly didn't care about. After that, she'd righted the chair and sat down to finish while Waylon had picked up beads and sorted them into their proper containers.

Now that they'd settled on a nightly maintenance regimen of fast, hard sex, she was cruising on stable. The meeting with her parents last night hadn't made her homicidal for bunnies. Mother had stressed the failure of the contractor to call about a timeline for getting the internet line in before winter hit. He wasn't returning her calls either. Both Mother and Father had demanded Shilo investigate why. Shilo thought that was exactly what Langdon wanted, to see their urgency.

It was early August and with hundreds of miles of cable to bury through dense woods, it wasn't looking like this year was the year of wifi for Ironhorse Falls. Langdon had strategically delayed them long enough that any further delays, likely orchestrated by him, would make all progress come to a halt once temps dipped below freezing.

And the maddening part? They shouldn't need this motherfucking internet. Sure, it was better than what they currently had, but they had options in place. Her colony hadn't been stuck in the Stone Age. Ironhorse Falls had satellites and cellular. But Covet controlled the towers sitting on their land, and weather made satellite connectivity difficult in the winter. Though the last year had seen some mysterious outages on perfectly cloud-free days.

No, Shilo was going to make Langdon wait. These lines and the massive amount of money it'd cost her people couldn't be their last options, it just couldn't.

It was time to stand up to Covet.

But it wasn't time to pressure Mother and Father about it.

Shilo sat up and swung her legs down. She was still naked, her body humming. Waylon never needed to stay long. No all-nighters. No clawing and shoving to get the level of stimulation her body demanded. Just him, giving her what she craved. She didn't wake up angry in the mornings with stomachaches from the previous night's slaughter of innocent creatures. Her meals now consisted of whatever magic Waylon created in the kitchen.

She jumped in the shower. The normalcy of the days could get addicting. As long as she wasn't stalling in her dealings with Langdon, she had an excuse to keep Waylon around. And times like these, she wasn't sure she could trust herself.

Toweling off and dressing in jean shorts and a pink tank top, she trotted downstairs. Her stomach stretched and woke up like she had just done, prepping for Waylon's attention. Her sex drive wasn't the only body part that liked having him around.

She inhaled, her mouth watering. Sausage and eggs, with diced bell peppers and cheese, all encased in a homemade wrap. The guy didn't have much to do while she worked and he'd been using his time to cook up a storm. If she didn't know him, she'd say it was his special ability. But she did know him. And she'd tasted the charred remains of the stir-fry attempt from two nights ago. The overabundance of soy sauce had required an extra three glasses of water to flush out the sodium and he'd spent an hour scrubbing the remains off the bottom of the pan.

But it was still better than any meal she could prep, so she hadn't complained, just prepared ham sandwiches while he'd aired out the bottom floor.

"Smells good."

"It is." Waylon was sitting at the table, reading the *Iron-horse Falls Daily*. Today he was wearing a navy-blue tee and his standard blue jeans. He looked better than Langdon in his expensive suits any day of the week, though she might be biased—she knew how Waylon could use that body.

What would he look like in a suit? A picture of Langdon

formed in her mind—same stance, same slicked-back dark hair, but instead of Langdon's haughtiness, Waylon's brooding eyes stared back. Weird.

Sliding into a chair, she was barely settled before she dug into her breakfast burrito. Three bites and it was gone. Waylon didn't look up as he slid a plate full of four other prepared burritos toward her. "Eat up. I've already had my share."

She mentally added more eggs to her list. And they could stop by the Monroes' and order another quarter pig for the freezer.

A burst of savory flavor exploded on her tongue. "These are good. What'd you do different?"

"Monterey jack cheese."

"Nice. It's good." She chuckled. "Unlike the coconut oil." Last week, he'd tried using coconut oil for a change. The oil had actually tasted like coconut instead of being flavorless.

"Weirdest-tasting eggs ever." He set the canister of coconut oil on the counter. "Hey, I was thinking since we won't use this for cooking, we could make lip balm and shit."

"Lip balm and shit?"

An adorable flush tinted his cheeks. "Christian's mate leaves magazines all over the break room. Waste not, want not and all that."

He was always full of surprises. One of the reasons she liked hanging out with him. "I know someone with a good supply of essential oils."

"We can head over there after I do dishes."

"I should just go on my own."

He shook his head and put the coconut oil back. "Never mind."

She swallowed her mouthful with her regret. She'd hurt his feelings. He'd been helping her for the last few weeks and now he thought she was ashamed of him.

"Waylon, I can't just show up at a friend's house with my bodyguard in tow. And it wouldn't be right to make you wait outside."

"I get it." He turned his back to fill the sink with dirty dishes.

She glanced down at her plate. Her appetite had left, but the food was too good to waste. She stuffed the rest in her mouth as the water ran and he added dish soap.

Last week, she'd needed a break from bending over her sewing table and had taken her sewing toolkits downstairs. She'd been in the middle of *Ocean's Eleven* when Waylon had plopped next to her.

"I love this movie," he'd said and begun sorting her faceted beads by color.

She'd known. It had been one of their favorites to watch while doing tedious, stationary tasks.

Her plate was empty. She took it to the sink and dropped it in, creeping close enough to Waylon inhale his heady pine scent. The coconut oil jar was to her right. She opened the top, stuck her finger in, then turned to Waylon and smeared it over his lips.

He jerked his head back. "What the hell?"

She grinned. "We'll leave to get the oils after dishes."

He maintained eye contact as he reached around her and dipped his finger into the jar.

"Don't you dare," she said, eyes narrowing.

His wicked smile sent electricity down to her toes. "Don't you want soft lips, Shilo?"

She feigned an indignant gasp. "Are you saying my lips aren't soft?"

His gaze dropped to her mouth. "They're as soft as down, and kissing them is like walking through the gates of heaven."

Her soft inhale wasn't fake this time. "Waylon."

He blinked, like snapping out of a trance. "After dishes. We'll go."

"Waylon."

"What, Shilo?" He scrubbed at a plate that was already clean.

Message received. "Nothing."

He was helping her stay sane. She couldn't let weeks of sex delude her into thinking they were more than an arrangement.

CHAPTER 11

"*How* ow many of these fucking jars do we have to fill?" Waylon grumbled. Shilo didn't have to know that he'd enjoyed the afternoon making a beauty product. A task he'd never imagined himself doing in his life, but half the fun had been spending time with Shilo.

Half the fun was betting who could spill the least amount of warmed, liquid lip balm into the small containers. It was like filling toy teacups. The kitchen was a mess of oils and the smell of lavender probably bloomed for a three-block radius.

"Um…" Shilo's gaze tracked the bucket of tiny lip balm containers. She bit her lip and turned away.

He narrowed his eyes. She was trying to keep from smiling.

The blame lay at his feet, but he couldn't bring himself to summon any anger. Once they'd driven to the other end of Ironhorse Falls and Shilo had explained to her curious friend what she was planning, it had been game on. Her friend, who was at least Weatherly's age, had been delighted, gushing that she hadn't had time to make any balm since her young was born.

Next thing he knew, he'd had instruction cards, jars of various oils from jojoba to almond, and bins of empty containers shoved in his hands. And the look on Shilo's face.

He knew that look. Her ability had fired up, sending familiar tingles through his body that he'd just assumed had always been from their chemistry. She was going to cook all these ingredients until they were gone—because her friend needed to reconnect with her past peddling natural beauty products before precocious young children had forced her to set it aside.

It was two a.m. and they were nearly done.

Shilo stretched her hands above her head and he averted his gaze from her jutting breasts.

"Go ahead and go to bed. I'll clean up."

She rolled her eyes at him. "I'm not leaving you with the cleanup. You pour—your hand's steadier, and I'll clean up."

He wasn't quite finished when she was done in the kitchen. She plopped on the couch and stared at the ceiling. Saying something would break the tranquility and he wanted to soak up the end to a pretty damn good day.

The last jar was filled without a drop spilled. He grinned. "Done."

There was no reply. Shilo's eyes were closed and her lips were parted. She was asleep.

He stacked their goods on the table, packed what was left of the loaned items, and treaded over to Shilo.

"Shilo?" he said quietly. "Wanna go to your room?"

She murmured and curled to her side as much as she could. It was clear who in this room had a night job.

Stooping, he wedged his arms under her and lifted. She curled into him, not completely waking up, but not lashing out from being startled.

She trusted him.

Carefully, he took her upstairs and laid her down on her bed. How he'd love to crawl into that bed with her and pretend the last five years hadn't happened. Pulling a hand-stitched quilt over her, he thought back to the first time he'd placed her here after his return. Their situation hadn't changed, but he couldn't help but feel that so much more had.

"I'D LIKE to go by Uncle Wolf's today."

Shilo nodded as she finished chewing breakfast. Neither she nor Waylon had spoken about the previous night, when he'd carried her to bed and tucked her in. The intimate and thoughtful action was beyond bodyguard duties, but then so was sorting her craft supplies and making lip balm.

Even her eggs tasted like lavender this morning. She couldn't decide if that was better or worse than coconut-flavored scrambled eggs.

"Sure, we can go," she said.

He hadn't asked to do anything while he was here. She was almost relieved to hear he wanted to visit the old cabin he'd grown up in. Waylon never talked about Uncle Wolf much, but she'd learned enough to know that Waylon had semi-enjoyed his time there. The cabin hadn't been a house of love, but there had been plenty to learn from the old hermit and Waylon had wanted to stay out of the spotlight.

As she polished off the rest of her breakfast and downed her juice, her mind returned to those early days. She'd catch glimpses of a rugged, wild male who wore tattered jeans and faded T-shirts. The clothes looked dirty, but only because they were old. The closer she got to him, the better he smelled. Soap and fresh air and forest, like he hand scrubbed his garments in pine needles. She hadn't been far off in her assumptions.

When she moved in for a "Hey, how are ya, haven't seen you around here much," he hadn't skittered away, afraid of her and all people. His brown gaze had been direct, intent, and the only time he'd broken eye contact was to brush his gaze down her shoulders, across the dangling hoop earrings she used to wear, and back again. He'd never ogled or leered, but his interest had been clear.

So was the fact that he was hers.

Had been hers.

You cannot mate him. We don't know his history—can't have him leading our people into the new world.

He's mine, Mother.

If he's yours, then we'll find a new successor.

The panic of being disowned had haunted her. Of course it hadn't bothered Waylon. One or both of his parents had dumped him in the middle of the woods, likely expecting him to die. The people of her colony had thrown around various tales and she'd listened intently, a young girl not knowing they were talking about the mate she hadn't met yet.

Maybe it was human poachers and they got his parents?

No, there were no signs of a fresh kill.

She'd listened, wide-eyed, at the doorway of pack meetings.

What if his own pack tried to kill him but didn't want to come back smelling like blood?

Who'd kill a young, fail, and then return without him?

No one had had an answer. They'd brainstormed Waylon's past and pondered what to do with him. No families had raised their hands to take in a young male with the Mother only knew what kind of temperament.

He's packless.

Then he's rogue. We kill him. Do what his own pack could not.

Father had cut that line of thinking off. *A child cannot be rogue.*

What if he grows into a teen who's bordering on feral?

Mother's voice rang loud; the practicality of her tone had stayed with Shilo. *Then we kill him, a full beheading. No rogues will come out of the Ironhorse Falls colony. If this young proves to be predisposed to going rogue, then he'll be swiftly dealt with, as we do.*

Mother and Father had barely waited forty-eight hours after Waylon had taken off before declaring him no longer one of the Ironhorse pack. Just like that, they were done with him.

That could've been Shilo, but she'd made her choice.

She doubted it was a coincidence Christian had found him and offered him status as one of theirs. Waylon had done nothing violent or wrong. He was a good male. Why did no one see it?

Why hadn't she tried to make them see it?

Bringing her empty dishes to the sink, she stopped long enough to wash them. Once they were on the drying rack, she grabbed her shoes. "Are we going on two legs or four?" Uncle Wolf's cabin was two miles from the colony and the trek would take them at least an hour in their human forms.

"Two," he said gruffly and headed for the door.

What was that about?

Oh, the nudity. Waylon probably wanted to walk through the cabin like this and not as a wolf. If they ran their wolves there and shifted back, they'd be without a stitch of clothing, which didn't usually bother their kind. But they were trying to keep as much emotional distance as they could and still have sex. It was a fine, nearly nonexistent line.

She stepped into her athletic shoes and followed him out, wearing her cotton-blend armor.

~

JUMPING from a jagged rock jutting out of a hillside, Waylon tried not to puff. Since he'd moved in with Shilo, he hadn't had to make this trek to town, had forgotten how strenuous it was. It was like Uncle Wolf had chosen the most rugged terrain to keep between him and civilization.

And knowing Uncle Wolf and his distrust of everyone, that was exactly what he'd done.

Shilo leaped down and caught up with Waylon. She hadn't broken a sweat while he'd perspired less after an hour-long boxing session. The forest canopy caught the brunt of the sun's rays, but the humidity had sunk below the trees. Clouds had gathered and were moving across the sun.

Shilo lifted her face and inhaled, a pleased smile spreading. "It's going to be a killer rain. Good. The crops need it. I think Mother was going to harvest some potatoes and leave some in front of my door."

Waylon grunted, trying to keep his breathing under control. Shilo pranced through the woods like a contemporary nymph who'd shunned her tutu for denim. Her hair hung down from a messy bun and her face glowed. The muscular build of her arms was a turn-on Waylon couldn't deny, and her ass... He couldn't go there.

Sex with her every night was going to his head. Both of them. Each day, he watched the clock. Was she in bed yet? How much more work before she called it a night and he could appear in her doorway? How long would her parents tiptoe around Langdon, giving him more time with Shilo?

Her parents. They tolerated him. Did they suspect he and Shilo were sleeping together again? They tried to be quiet.

He was fast—and thorough. But if he lingered, the part of his brain that was more man than shifter started thinking about the what-ifs. What if her mother lightened up? What if Langdon lost interest in Ironhorse Falls? What if Shilo accepted him?

Weatherly and Shilene weren't any friendlier than before, but they'd reverted to their previous aloofness when it came to him. They ignored him during the gatherings, but the burn of their stare stabbed between his shoulder blades when they thought he wasn't paying attention.

For two leaders who treated the Covet situation with kid gloves, they seemed oddly comfortable shoving Shilo at Langdon any chance they got.

Waylon scowled at his boots as he stepped through the fallen branches and the tall grasses that survived deep in the woods. Should he bring up the observation with Shilo? Had she noticed herself?

The contractor hasn't called. You should set up another meeting with Langdon.

It'd been three weeks since that meeting. Waylon's experience watching Christian run the bar was that humans delayed their projects all the time. Langdon probably was interfering, but her parents were rushing to act just how he wanted them to, shoving her in front of Langdon like some virginal peace offering.

"Oh my gosh. I see it." Shilo pointed to the faded wood cabin in the distance. The lone stone wall with the crumbling chimney had seen better days, but other than a vine that accepted the challenge of encompassing the entire structure, it looked the same.

He could almost hear Uncle Wolf's rumbling voice. *Don't waste the emotion*, he'd said when eight-year-old Waylon had cried after breaking his leg. *Survival should be instinctual, not a mystery.* That was during a nasty blizzard that had kept them holed up for a month. Waylon had panicked about food sources and supplies. *The earth provides. She doesn't hold our fucking hand and read us the instruction manual as a bedtime story.*

The reluctant guardian. Uncle Wolf had a head of gray hair in Waylon's earliest memory of him, but he'd never said how old he was. Centuries. He'd answered few of Waylon's questions over the years. Yes, he had mated. No, she wasn't alive. But the question of whether he had young of his own had ended badly. Uncle Wolf had descended into a melancholic state that had lasted for two weeks, leaving Waylon to prepare all the food at ten years old. He hadn't been old enough to venture into town on his own, and even if he had been, there'd been no money. Waylon had hunted as a wolf and turned his one successful kill into a stew that had lasted the first week.

The second week, he'd picked greens from the garden to steam but hadn't realized he'd picked rhubarb greens and poisoned them both.

The next time you try to kill me, boy, use a blade, not a supper that tastes like shit before it makes me regret living to see the next day. Then he'd laughed, the first sign Uncle Wolf had busted out of his rut. *If shifters could die from poisoning, I'd have offed myself with liquor long ago.*

Reaching the cabin, Waylon forced the memories back. The pull of this place had been weighing on him since he'd returned to Ironhorse Falls.

Shilo circled the small structure. "Is it safe to go inside?"

"I'll go first." The cabin collapsing on them wouldn't kill them, but it'd suck to be stranded under a pile of rubble with no way to call for help.

He tried the doorknob. Uncle Wolf had never believed in locks. *If they want to finish the job, they can come and get me. I got nothing to steal.*

Waylon had always thought that if someone ventured out this far, they weren't here to take anything, but it didn't mean their reason was a good one. But until he'd rented the loft over the offices, he hadn't had a place of his own to lock, so he hadn't argued with the old man.

The familiar smell hit him, washing glimpses of the past over him. Uncle Wolf looming over him on his pine-bough mat, growling at him to wake up. Failing over and over to start a fire one wet spring when the fire pit had flooded until Uncle Wolf rolled his eyes and withdrew a Bic from a box of cigars he'd seemed to produce from thin air. Prepping skins of the wild game they caught to use as rugs half the year when stepping on a cold wood floor would leave him shivering for hours. Cleaning their guns after target practice.

Damn, Waylon had hated cleaning guns. But Uncle Wolf had made sure he excelled at physical fighting and target practice. At first, Waylon had thought it was for the hunting, but no. *Again, boy. Center mass. Again, boy. You only hit four out of five.*

Uncle Wolf would go to town and trade pelts for lead. But Waylon didn't mind. It beat the boredom and he'd rather lose to the male on targets than get his ass walloped in hand-to-hand. Uncle Wolf had had a mean left hook.

Watch your peripherals, kid. Human or wolf, fight smart.

"Wow." Shilo eased past him as he was lost to his memories. "It really hasn't changed."

Oh, it had. Dust covered every surface, from the smooth, varnished tree-stump end table to the hand-carved mantle above the fireplace. Sun streamed through the windows, somehow still intact. Particles filtered through the beams, casting an overlay over his childhood home. Even the firearms he'd used for hunting and target practice had lost their shine. Part of him felt compelled to sit down and clean them.

Waylon's steps landed heavy on the wood planks, leaving footprints in the grit that had blown in over the years. He went to his old bedroom, an eight-by-eight addition Uncle Wolf had constructed after Waylon had moved in. The neatly sewn mat was still on the floor. Handcrafted bins that had functioned as his dresser were empty by the wall. All his possessions, nothing but a backpack of clothing, had moved out with him.

Being mates doesn't solve every problem between a couple. Her parents will never think you're worthy.

Then I'll have to find out who I am so they can trust me.

Uncle Wolf snorted, his eyes flashing with a feeling Waylon couldn't identify. *You'd better hope they never find out who you are.*

Waylon had asked what that meant, but Uncle Wolf had shucked his canvas trousers, shifted, and never come back. The next time Waylon had seen him, he'd been dead on the stoop.

What had Waylon expected? Uncle Wolf hadn't been a dying-of-old-age male. Waylon rubbed his chest.

"It wasn't your fault." Shilo hadn't missed the move. "Not even we live forever. You staying here wouldn't have changed that. He had unfinished business and he waited until you were on your own."

Waylon hadn't said a word since they'd arrived. His throat was clogged with emotion, and the longing to know who he was and where he'd come from charged back. Without Uncle Wolf, Waylon was adrift in the world, back to the same state he'd been in as a little boy before he'd gazed up at a scraggly old shifter who'd grudgingly taken him in. He'd had a home with Uncle Wolf, then again with Shilo.

And he'd lost both of them.

He wandered to the next room, the door only feet away. This space was larger, rectangular and nearly as sparse.

Before Waylon's addition, it had been open to the rest of the cabin. But Uncle Wolf had walled it off. He'd wile hours away in there. Waylon had never known what the male had been up to.

Waylon walked in. He ran a finger over the furniture Uncle Wolf had carved and buffed out of fallen pine. So much work, so many hours put into pieces that would eventually rot out here, unused and unappreciated.

"Not even a dream catcher." Shilo skimmed her fingers over the bare log walls. "That's odd in Ironhorse Falls. Even those without native ancestry have 'em."

"He made it clear he wasn't from here. He pledged his allegiance to your pack only to be left alone."

"I always assumed he'd been born and raised around here. He knew too much about living off the land, this land, to have moved from anywhere else."

Waylon nodded. "I guess we'll never know." He stepped to the side to check the clothing bins, the urge to have just one memento of the only father he'd known driving him.

He hadn't even grabbed a carving when he'd left. At the time, he'd just felt abandoned by everyone.

He'd never asked Shilo what she'd done with the carvings. That would've been too...intimate. If she still had them, the knowledge might disrupt their little arrangement. And if she'd burned them... That would disrupt their arrangement, too.

A shelf of tiny carved figures was mounted against the far wall. He stepped toward it.

A board creaked.

"Huh, I'm surprised he didn't fix this." Waylon put pressure on it again. The groan was louder than any other board in the house.

"Maybe it was just one of those things he never got around to."

"Yeah." Waylon couldn't quit with the board. There was no basement and he doubted there was even a subfloor, but this piece sank like nothing was underneath it. He dropped to his knees.

Shilo squatted down with him. "A hiding spot?"

"Maybe, but I gotta see."

He pushed and pressed along the length of the plank. At the end, he spotted an odd piece that didn't blend. Palpating it, he frowned. Putty?

Peeling it away revealed a well-worn screw. The other planks had two screws in each end, but this had a screw that looked like it was frequently removed.

Waylon jumped up and dug in a bin. Uncle Wolf's whittling tools. He grabbed one with a small blade that could fit into the screwhead.

The screw was out in seconds. He pulled the wood away to reveal a small, square hole dug into the dirt. The cigar box sat inside.

"Huh," Waylon said again. He dug the box out, and both he and Shilo sat back on their butts. She scooted close. He lifted the lid and chuckled. The Bic. He lifted it out and set it on the floor. "This thing saved our asses more than once. I never thought about where he kept the box, just that he had the lighter when we needed it."

Two other things were inside. A stone and a picture of a happy couple with a little baby. The color had faded and the box had suffered water damage that had seeped into the photo.

Shilo gasped. "He had a family."

Waylon squinted at the picture. "I don't think that's Uncle Wolf." The male in the photo had hair and a bushy beard, but it wasn't gray. The picture itself was newer than the Polaroid years. Waylon turned it over. The date was printed on the back.

"That means the kid's not much older than me." Shilo turned the photo back over. "No, that isn't Uncle Wolf."

"The date might just be when the picture was printed. It could've been taken earlier and not developed."

Shilo pointed at the top the woman was wearing. "They're both dressed more modern than my father."

"All the colonies dress more modern than Weatherly."

She giggled. "True. I wish he'd update, but then I couldn't sew him bell-bottoms anymore."

Waylon inspected the couple. They both had dark hair. Hers was long and draped over one shoulder and while she was smiling, her eyes were tired. On the surface, they were happy, at least for the split second the shutter opened and closed. His eyes were hard, fathomless, his grip on the baby tight. Her hand came around, not overlapping his, but gripping the baby's foot like she was hanging on for all it was worth.

"They were having problems," Waylon said.

"Yeah." Shilo tilted her head. "I see it now, too. I wonder if they're still alive. Son? Daughter of Uncle Wolf?"

"Or was he legitimately an uncle?" No, that didn't feel right. "I bet he used the moniker to stay hidden. No one would think of him as a father."

"But why would he want to stay hidden?"

Wasn't that the million-dollar question. Was Uncle Wolf a rich recluse who shunned the modern world? Or just a recluse who couldn't function in the modern world?

He'd had a family. He wouldn't hide and hold on to a photo like this otherwise.

Who had left first? Uncle Wolf, or the people in the photo?

"I guess we'll never know the story." Waylon tucked the photo and the Bic under his arm and stood up. Shilo rose and stretched.

Suddenly, what they'd found didn't matter. Her body was sun-kissed and her sweet-clover scent teased his nose.

He grabbed her hand and pulled her toward his old room.

"Oh, good idea," she said, apparently sensing his desire. "I'm tired of being quiet."

CHAPTER 12

*W*ith her legs wrapped around him, he pushed inside. Waylon's eyes rolled back in his head. Morning, noon, and night he could be inside of Shilo. Their long separation had made the need stronger, like nature's way of keeping them from parting again.

If only it were possible.

She rocked her hips up. After stripping down in a frenzy, they'd bypassed kissing and fallen together on the mat. Over the last few weeks, he'd done everything to her but claim her.

The urge was getting harder to resist. He rocked out and thrust in. She arched her back, shoving her breasts in his face and baring her neck.

The urge was getting harder for her, too.

"Why the fuck can't we work things out?" he panted. This wasn't the time for a relationship talk, but being back at the cabin had exposed his emotions.

His childhood was a mystery and he was alone in the world. Alone except for his mate underneath him. Why couldn't he be with his mate the way they were meant to be?

She hitched her knees up and gripped his ass, her fingernails digging into his skin. He fucking loved it.

"Because we're both too stubborn," she gasped. "I'm close. I can't believe how fast you can get me off."

He could say the same.

Instead he slowed and dropped himself to his elbows. Lowering his head by her ear, he said, "Why can't we work on it? We've got time, right?"

She stopped rocking her hips and met his gaze. "Are you...are you serious?"

Stroking her hair, he brushed a kiss across her pink lips. "I've missed you. And these last few weeks have been..."

"A relief?"

He smiled. "Because you finally get cooked meals?"

She grinned, biting her lower lip. "That's nice, too." Her expression turned serious. "We still have the same problems. I can't run out and mate you until we resolve them."

"I'll keep my fangs to myself?"

He wanted to coax a smile from her, but she feathered her hand along his hair. "I want to know you won't leave me when we hit the next rough patch."

Her words had a physical punch. He sucked in air. Had he been in the wrong to walk away? "I won't leave you. But the succession thing... I'm not going to be strung along."

"I'll work on the home front if you stay by my side and talk me down from the insanity ledge."

He dropped his head to kiss her before asking, "We're a thing again?"

Cupping his face, she gazed solemnly into his eyes. "We're a thing again." She rocked her hips into him. "I think that calls for make-up sex."

"We have five years to make up for, princess." The next kiss was longer, and he poured his feelings into it. Maybe it was finding a hidden part of Uncle Wolf that had opened him up to hoping for a future with Shilo again. Knowing that the old man had hidden his past while Waylon had none, no one wondering who Uncle Wolf was, how he'd ended up— Waylon didn't want that to be him.

But his future was with her. Shilo leaned on him, but it wasn't her current state of dependency that tied him to her. He didn't need an ego stroking. It was the feeling of home, of belonging that she provided.

It was why it hurt so much when she'd acquiesced to her parents' wishes.

Shoving the past and the concerns of the future out of his mind, he concentrated on the present. On the female writhing underneath him. On being able to finally acknowledge that his life was a shell without her.

This time was going to be different.

SPREADING OUT THE TRADITIONAL DRESS, Shilo smoothed all the wrinkles and double-checked the bead attachments. These dresses weren't for show. They'd get danced in with all the twirling, bouncing, and shimmying that went with a powwow.

Once a month, members of the colony gathered for the casual trade of skills and goods. Orders were made as the attendees drank coffee and socialized. It was mostly a party for those who didn't party.

Waylon stood off to the side. For the last few days, in public, they were back to merely being in the same orbit. He guarded her, she carried on like he wasn't there.

In private, she clung to him and pretended he wouldn't have to leave her bed by morning.

A woman bounded up, her long black hair pulled back in a clip. Dyani, one of the human mates of the colony, was the proud owner of the dress. "Oh, this was just like I wore when I was a girl." She walked a circle around the table, inspecting every inch of it. "I could never have even imagined this level of beadwork."

That was her gift. Before Shilo had discovered the level of design she was capable of, the colony had done their own period pieces. Any elders passed their wisdom on and the members struggled with the literal definition of traditional. But one thing stayed the same: time moved forward. Memories grew foggier, details more clouded, and human mates lost touch with the world they'd once known—the brittle curse of a human mate outliving their loved ones and moving on with shifterkind. As isolated as Ironhorse Falls was, it could be harder to cling to the past, and losing one's history wasn't always a good thing.

Mother's goal with all the packs was to preserve as many customs and ceremonies as they could. Matings were 100 percent shifter. No marriages, no weddings. They observed Christmas, and the few Jewish mates they had in the colony had taught them about Hanukah. Valentine's Day was fun and the Fourth of July could get wild. But the annual powwow was a tradition that had been around for almost a century. The event took place in September and had morphed into the final goodbye to summer as the colony turned toward planning for the brutal winters.

It was during one meeting when Shilo had been thirteen that a pack leader had detailed moccasins his mate had been wearing when he'd met her. He'd recited the details of the dye colors and porcupine-bristle decorations. Shilo had hunted a porcupine that evening, risking quills in her muzzle, and crafted a pair that had made a proud shifter weep openly.

The outfit she'd produced had shocked the members of the colony. The next year, a friend had asked for one. Soon, she was constructing vibrant outfits with little guidance on the variations between native peoples. She just knew. The same happened when she'd quilted a wall hanging for a relatively new mate who'd just lost his German mother.

As for her shifter side, she could sew any fur that came her way into the finest stole or coat, which they may have to revert to. As rural as they were, residents managed to buy Columbia or North Face winter outerwear, but if Passage Lake succeeded at cutting them off entirely, the colony might need to unearth those old skills because she wouldn't be able to keep up with demand.

An elderly female shuffled her way.

"Hey, Olga. How's it going?"

Olga was graying and getting slower. She was a human mate, but she'd been a member of the Ironhorse pack for longer than many of their members had been alive. Her floral dresses with laces at the hems were cute as a button and the thick white orthopedic shoes she wore didn't slow her down. It was a fool who underestimated Olga.

"Another masterpiece, Ms. Ironhorse." Olga never called her Shilo, and her words still had traces of a Norwegian accent. A little heavier stress on a consonant here, a drawn-out vowel there.

"Thank you." It was high praise. The older woman never gave out false compliments.

Olga dug into a little pouch she always had secured around her waist. She produced a fist full of neatly folded bills. "With Bergen's help, I saved up some money."

"Oh?" Shilo's interest skyrocketed. The family was notoriously frugal but some of the best producers in the colony. Working the soil with their hands and not machinery meant they didn't spend what they earned lightly.

"I've been having dreams of home. It's been so long..." Her bright-blue eyes turned melancholy. "I'd like my own traditional dress. When my time comes, I want to go wearing the garb of my homeland."

Having been born a shifter, in a shifter colony, Shilo was in awe of those who sacrificed everything they knew for the love of their mate. It'd been an impossible task for her. "I will make any dress you want."

Olga pulled out a nearby chair. Her gaze was unfocused and a haunting smile graced her lips. "I want a festival dress, a *bunad*."

Shilo asked a few questions on coloring and style. The more Olga described the type of dress she wanted, the easier Shilo formed a mental image. An A-line tucked in at the waist, flowing to the ankle. Beading starting at the collar, traveling down the bodice into an explosion on the skirt. Though this was her first Norwegian design, the image in her head was fully realized down to the colors and types of beads she'd use.

"Do you want me to sketch it out for you before I start?" she asked. "And when would you like it by?"

Olga shook her head and stood, taking an extra second to steady herself. "You always take good care of us. I trust your creation. And…as soon as possible, please."

Shilo smiled but fiddled with the craft box she packed in case there were any wardrobe issues caused en route. *Take good care of us.* By crafting. How much did that help? She was supposed to the future leader.

A brush across her nape made her look over her shoulder. Waylon's chiding gaze was on her. He'd probably heard Olga's comment and guessed what she was thinking. They shared their insecurity about their inferior mental abilities.

Shilo closed her craft tackle box and flattened her hands on the material. After smoothing invisible creases out of the garment, she neatly folded it for Dyani to take home.

She hefted her gear. "I want to get started on this order

for Olga." The frequent trips to Freemont had set her behind. Olga never asked for much, so if she wanted the dress ASAP, she'd get it ASAP.

Waylon was her shadow out of the building. He still received curious stares, but the hostility had faded. He was clearly intent on his duty to watch her, and for now, that was good enough for them.

But it didn't explain why Waylon wasn't welcome in Iron-horse Falls. Even before he'd left her, residents hadn't gone out of their way to be friendly. Uncle Wolf had been treated better, despite being the colony recluse who hated to talk to anyone.

In the Jeep, he paused before he threw the vehicle in gear. "When are we talking to your parents?"

She was surprised he'd waited this long to ask. "Charlie and Cass's funeral is this weekend. Can we wait until after that?" She'd be emotionally wrecked and need time to recover before she unearthed old arguments that had never seemed to go anywhere.

Waylon's stare was lingering and lacked hostility. Disappointment? "After the funeral then."

"Good. And now, I need a run in the woods before I call that damn contractor tomorrow." She'd put the discussion with her parents off for at least another week. It was her big accomplishment of the day.

CHAPTER 13

The send-off for his old friends was peaceful, unlike their deaths. He wished he could've done his own inspection of the crime scene, but he didn't have any special skills or possess the same training as the Guardians. He had to trust what they found. Or in this case, what they hadn't found.

The Guardian who'd escorted the bodies to Ironhorse Falls had discussed the results of their investigation with Weatherly and Shilene. Shilo and Waylon had been in the room and that was it. The information would get disseminated down to the individual pack leaders—after the Ironhorses decided on what details to keep to themselves.

But it was unnecessary. The Guardians had found nothing. The couple had sat still while they were bled out and beheaded. No clues. No camera footage. No scents, nothing out of place, no evidence of any kind.

How convenient.

Shilene tied up her speech, her strong, firm voice carrying on the wind to the hundreds of people that had showed. Funny how two of the most well-liked shifters in Ironhorse Falls had befriended him.

Waylon clasped his hands in front of him. The ceremony wasn't fancy, but he felt like he stood out in the only clothes he'd packed: T-shirt and jeans. At least he had a black pair of each. He glanced up at Shilo, wanting to do nothing more than hug her shaking body close to him as she silently cried for her lost friends. But he stood behind the rest of the crowd, routinely scanning familiar and unfamiliar faces alike. Only grief hung in the air, no hostility, not even toward him.

As everyone wandered down the path to the parking lot, he kept Shilo in his peripheral. She meandered down the trail with her parents. Breaking off to go to the Jeep, she waved to her parents and said, "See you at the house."

He held the door open for her, then crawled in on his side. The line of cars wasn't as long it would've seemed from the crowd. Several had walked from town, many others carpooling. Not many shifted and ran. So many human mates had made them a more chaste colony than others. Even his own time among humans had given him a case of modesty.

The drive down the hill and winding around town was quiet. He'd sat with Shilo on his lap last night as they'd shared stories of the old times with Charlie and Cass. Grill outs. Runs to the nearby falls Ironhorse Falls was named for. Movie nights.

Car salesmen. They'd been in Freemont how long, and he hadn't known they were there? If he'd known, would he have contacted them or been too afraid to cross paths with Shilo?

Water under the bridge. He was with Shilo now. That was what mattered.

She would talk to her parents, and no matter how it turned out, he was here to stay.

Her parents were in a Range Rover in front of them. They slowed and Shilo sat forward. "What the fuck are they doing here?"

Waylon was intent on the vehicle in front of him; he hadn't glanced up at the house. In front was a black Escalade, and waiting at the landing, with his sharply creased trousers and his foot resting on the lower step, was Langdon Covet. His expression was placid but his gaze intense as it switched from the Range Rover to the Jeep. A calculating gleam entered his eye as he caught sight of Shilo. It was wiped out by a hard edge when he looked at Waylon.

Paulie stood by the Escalade, still in his overalls, like a mechanic-slash-bouncer, whatever the occasion called for. Another male and a female got out as they approached. The same from the meeting in Freemont, Oscar and Brynley. Weatherly stopped behind the Escalade, but Waylon continued past to the back of the house.

"What are you doing?" Shilo muttered, moving her lips as little as possible. Yeah, he wouldn't put it past the fuckers to read lips, either.

"They're looking to throw us off. We'll do the same."

He parked in his normal spot and they got out. Shilo was charging to the door, but he jogged toward her.

"Take your time. Saunter in. You have the power here, whether Langdon thinks that's true or not. Show him that this is your territory."

Determination rippled through her and she slowed.

They strode in. Shilo played her part well.

She entered with a smile and took her standard chair at the table. Waylon took his normal post. Langdon pretended Waylon didn't exist, but a muscle in the male's jaw tensed and his expression hardened.

Paulie made no attempts to feign ignorance. He glared openly. Oscar and Brynley were dressed like Langdon understudies. Pressed slacks. Blazer. Dark colors. All they needed were shades and they could be extras in a cop drama.

Weatherly's pride shone through his eyes, but Shilene bristled with annoyance. At her daughter or at the unannounced visitors?

Langdon sat forward, his elbows on the table, his hands clasped. His suit jacket stretched enough around his frame to show off the bulge of his muscles. A tailoring effect, no doubt. Arrogant prick. He used every advantage. "Now that we're all here, I can get started. I have a proposal that will help your colony."

Shilene tipped her head, her expression obviously an unspoken *You're kidding me, right?*

"I've listened to Shilo's troubles over the years. I think I can help. Human contractors don't take her seriously. I hate to say...they almost look to me for guidance."

Waylon wanted to cough "bullshit" into his hand. Did Langdon really think they were buying his sincere act?

"And to touch on a sensitive subject, I've heard about the unfortunate circumstances of Shilo's mate."

Waylon stepped forward. He'd take that fucker down a notch—by smashing his fist in the male's nose. Shilene cut off his advance with a sharp glare. Paulie angled himself to block Langdon.

As for Langdon, the smug bastard, he remained above it all. "I will mate Shilo and unite our packs."

Shilo snorted a laugh. Waylon didn't know if anyone else made a sound, he couldn't hear past the pounding heartbeat in his ears. The male wanted to mate Waylon's female?

No. Never.

Shilo would set them straight about her "unfortunate" mating circumstances.

All she said was, "I'm not mating you."

Langdon spared her a glance. "But it's not entirely up to you, Shilo. Your parents are in charge."

Electricity charged through the room.

Weatherly was shaking his head, but Shilene spoke. "And if we decline?"

Langdon parted his hands in a what-can-I-do gesture. "I imagine it'll continue to be an uphill battle for Shilo as your negotiator. It certainly doesn't inspire confidence in her ability to lead if even humans can't take her seriously." He paused, the effect pure theater. "The rest of the colony will start to doubt her ability to lead. I've already heard rumors."

"That you started?" The words burst out of Waylon before he could stop them.

Langdon cast him a cool look. Brynley stiffened, her gaze darting around the room. Shilene's expression was full of daggers and death wishes.

When was Shilo going to tell them that she was off the market?

"We'll think about it," Weatherly said. Shilene nodded.

A delaying tactic. Had to be.

Langdon sucked in his lower lip and let it out slowly, flashing a hint of fang in the process. "I'm afraid I can't afford to give you that long. I'm putting my own mating status on the line, and I can't hang in limbo."

Waylon's vision tunneled, going cloudy around the edges. All he had to do was chew through the male's neck and this would be over. He wanted to dive into Shilo's head and tell her to announce that she was taken, but she didn't need the distraction.

"One week," Langdon said.

"One month," Shilene countered.

Shilo's head bobbed back and forth like she was a spectator at the world's sickest tennis match.

"Two weeks and my offer is withdrawn. I'm sure you

could use my help with the contractors. I'd hate for increased delays this close to winter."

Waylon had to be throwing off waves of aggression. He planted his feet and fisted his hands, but he kept his back against the wall. It was either that or tear that stupid smirk off Paulie's face.

"Internet isn't critical to our survival," Weatherly said.

"It makes it easier to notify suppliers that your food shipments can't make it through the snow." Langdon leveled his dark gaze on Shilo. "It'd make you downright...crazy. That'd be hard for you, Shilo. Right? With the impending rogue madness descending."

Shilo sucked in a breath.

Cold slammed into Waylon's chest. How the hell did that jackass know about Shilo's mental state?

Her parents were as stiff as icicles on a frigid winter day.

Langdon rose, smoothed down his jacket, and strode out the door, his three cronies on his heels. His departure lacked all the respect due to the pack leaders in the room.

No one said a word until they sensed the Covet members were gone.

"Is it true?" Shilene's voice shook. "You feel the madness?"

"I'm handling it. What are we going to do?" Shilo was addressing her parents.

Shilo. Was addressing. Her parents.

"I hope you mean what are you going to do when you turn him down," Waylon growled.

Shilo shot him a censoring stare over her shoulder. He gave her a *what the fuck* look right back.

"This doesn't involve you, Wolf," Shilene said.

"How can you say that?" Waylon shook his head. "We'd be mated already if it weren't for you and you wouldn't be dealing with this fucking power trip of Langdon's. But, hey, let's forget the 'you mate him, and we'll disown you' threat, I'm here as her guard—against *Langdon*."

"That's enough, Wolf." Weatherly stood, his chest puffed out. "Our pack business does not involve you. Our daughter made her decision."

Waylon's gaze darted back to Shilo. Her leg was crossed over the other and bouncing, and her arms were folded across her chest as she glowered at the wall across from her.

If not now, when was "the talk" with her parents supposed to happen? Where was the adamant denial that she would mate Langdon?

Where was the mate who had his back when he needed her?

He was done here.

∿

SHILO SQUEEZED her eyes shut when Waylon left on a wave of fury. The utter dejection in his scent was hard for her to process.

She needed his support now more than ever, not to resurrect an old fight. Langdon had calmly and calculatingly threatened her entire colony if she didn't mate him. Announcing that she was now back with her mate would put her colony in the position of an imminent fight. Her people were strong, but they'd worked so hard to survive as isolated as they were, a fight would decimate them. Any survivors would have to move to larger, more stable colonies.

And if she mated Langdon? A shudder swept through her. How long before her parents met with some happy accident that left the Ironhorse Falls colony to her, and there was Langdon at her side?

No, she wouldn't be standing by Langdon's side anytime soon—or ever. Her refusal would have to be planned, prepped for, starting with her parents. She couldn't just blurt out to them that her status with Waylon had changed until she'd discussed her assumptions with him first.

The situation they found themselves in wasn't sudden. Langdon had been planning this longer and more thoroughly than any of them could've guessed. He'd set it all up. Slowly, meticulously. Like Waylon had said, he'd put the bait in front of Shilo to determine how unstable she was becoming.

Now that she'd pulled back and sought refuge in her natural mate's arms, Langdon had upped his game. And it was driving Waylon away, like Langdon probably wanted.

Her parents were talking but she hadn't heard a thing they said.

"I need to talk to him." Shilo nearly tipped her seat over and charged down the hall, the fear that he'd be gone when she went looking for him making her clumsy.

Her parents didn't chase her. They'd stay and strategize, and truthfully, Shilo wasn't sure she'd like what they came up with. She had to talk to Waylon.

In her own part of the house, she went straight to the guest room and barreled into Waylon's chest as he was coming out. His backpack was slung over his shoulder.

The sight just plain pissed her off. She shoved him back into the room and slammed the door behind her. "Why are you leaving?"

"I'm not doing this again, Shilo."

"Damn it, Waylon. Is that going to be your first instinct the rest of our lives? To just fucking leave when we hit a rough patch?"

Indecision crossed his face. "There's no 'we' right now. Langdon made a claim on you and you didn't even look at me."

"Excuse me if I was a little taken aback trying to wrap my mind around being negotiated over like livestock. We can't figure this out if you take off—again." She planted her hands on her hips, still blocking the door. Hurt from the last time he left wound its way around her heart. Why was she that easy for him to abandon?

"Don't." He dropped the backpack to the floor.

She lifted her gaze to his. "Don't what?"

"Don't make me feel like the bad guy, Shilo. We're both in this, but right now I feel like the only one who supports *us*."

She stalked toward him and poked him in the shoulder. "I support us. But I can't just parade around Ironhorse Falls as if I don't have responsibilities. I'm going to tell my parents—*we're* going to tell my parents, but after Langdon stormed in here was not the time." She poked him again. "He's up to something, and for some reason, Mother and Father aren't proactive when it comes to him. All I have to figure this out, to figure him out, is you."

She went to poke him again, but he grabbed her finger. Some of the fury had drained out of his eyes. He kissed her fingertip, and she twisted her hand out of his grip. The mental exhaustion brought on by the events of the day weighed her down. She flopped on the bed with her legs hanging over the end.

"I can't believe you think I'd mate Langdon." How could he think she'd entertain that?

"If that's what your parents really wanted in the name of preserving the colony." Waylon's footsteps were barely audible as he crossed to stand at her knees. "What if they order you to mate someone else? They'd take you off the market and restore your sanity."

Oh God. Mother and Father would totally do something like that. What *would* she do? She'd gone along with everything they wanted. She'd fought off the early descent into madness out of her need to please them. Would she mate someone else and willingly cut Waylon out of her life?

"I want you," she said stubbornly, like that was going to solve everything.

"We both want each other. And what about my developing power? It's not going to impress them. I mean, sensing when others are using their skills? And you feel like yours is useless. Mine provides no offensive abilities and is mildly defensive at best when it comes to fighting Langdon."

"You've done more against Langdon with your attitude and the shit you've said to him than my entire colony has done."

He thought a moment, then gave a curt nod. "Are we willing to fight for each other?"

She patted the bed next to her. He sat and lay back in the same position she was in.

"I'm not going to mate anyone else." The truth in her quiet words rang between them. "I'm *not* going to mate anyone else," she said again. Sweet Mother, that felt good.

"Do you want to mate me more than you want to belong to the colony? Because that's what it might come to. Do you love me?"

She turned her head. He was staring at her. The *l* word hadn't been said since he'd returned. "Do you love me?" she returned.

"I never stopped."

"I never stopped either."

"Maybe I should rephrase that," he said. "Do you trust me?"

She rolled up to lean on her elbow. "What's that supposed to mean?"

"I'm the abandoned kid who was raised by the town oddball. No one trusted me."

"I did. I do." She leaned down to kiss him, but he set a big hand on her shoulder.

"If you give me your word, the sun will rise and set with

you. I will never leave your side, and I'll always be yours. But I can't do that and have you change your mind when you tell your parents about us, or when the people here ask you why in the world you're with me. Cuz I'm telling you right now, the reason why I left was because if they'd asked, you'd have mated someone else and I'd have had to kill him. And then you'd have hated me forever."

Would she have done that? She couldn't say. What had held her back at the time? Was it a lack of respect, of trust that he could be everything she needed even if no one else thought so?

She thought back to earlier when he'd walked out. She hadn't trusted that he'd stay and support her, and he hadn't trusted that she wasn't entertaining the idea of acquiescing to her parents. They had all the fiery passion in the world but not enough faith in each other. It was time to rectify that.

Swinging her leg over him, she straddled him and cupped his face. "You're mine."

Desire flared in his eyes, but he didn't wrap his arms around her. He was holding back. Could she blame him? His steadfast devotion had been thrown in his face. Because he'd been hers and hers alone, she'd taken him for granted until he'd become disposable in her mind.

Her stomach curdled. A tear rolled down her cheek. "It was my fault."

The admission was a revelation. Her fault. All of it. And in some messed up way, she'd put her people at greater risk. Langdon was exploiting her weakness, which was losing Waylon.

More tears rolled down her cheeks. "I was so mad at you, but I should've been furious at me." The sobs started. She tried to hold them back, but when his eyes started glistening, the dam broke.

"Shh." He drew her down and curled her into her arms. "A

relationship takes two. You should've fought, I should've stayed."

"I m-m-missed you."

He kissed the top of her head. "I tried not to sleep or I'd dream of you."

After a minute her crying quieted. She looked at his handsome face. The way his hair was brushed back from lying down, how he was holding her. That body that knew exactly what she wanted and how she needed it.

How could she prove that she was ready for the next step?

It was obvious. He was her mate. "Claim me."

CHAPTER 14

*H*is mouth was hanging open, but no sound came out.

"Claim me," she said again.

He'd definitely heard her correctly.

All those years, they'd known they were mates, but the constant disapproval had kept her from outright asking him to claim her. He'd always known that she'd needed an out, that being torn between him and everyone else would eventually come to a head, and it had. She'd given him little signs she wanted him to give her the bite that would signal to every other male to back the hell off, but their whole relationship had been about not calling attention to themselves.

A claim would scream for attention without saying a word. Was she serious?

The scent of her desire clogged the room. His cock rose to answer her need. Yes, she meant it.

But now wasn't the time. "We tell your parents first."

The desire fell like a boulder. "You want to wait?"

He rolled over on top of her. "No, but I don't want to go

from me leaving for five years because you didn't stand up to them to me marking you and making them worry we'll go ahead and bond before this Covet thing is taken care of. You care what they think. I can wait until you tell them." *I don't want to be a mistake.*

A frown creased her brow and the plummet of desire in the room made it hard to know if she was considering what he was saying, or if this moment was a fluke and he'd pissed her off too bad to go back to considering forever together.

He couldn't leave her again. For the last couple of weeks, he'd been whole for once. He'd...had fun. They'd watched movies, run through the woods, cuddled. And the constant tension and restlessness that had plagued him were gone. Even before the moment they'd tentatively recommitted at Uncle Wolf's cabin, he'd still felt a level of peace he hadn't experienced in years.

He selfishly didn't want to go back. While he didn't want to be the reason she was stressed out about broadcasting their growing reconnection, he also didn't want to go back to the lonely existence of the last few years.

"Let's go tell them." She wiggled enough to mainline blood back to his privates while she got out from under him. Straightening her clothes and smoothing her hair, she went to the door.

"Now?" Was he ready? Without so much as a claim, much less a full bond, they were still reversible. And he could still lose her.

"Yep. I'm an adult, and yes, I'm under their tutelage and authority. While the matter between you and me is my business, I don't get the luxury of thinking it doesn't affect the future of the colony. You're right—we can't do this in secret. Whether Mother and Father approve of it or not, it's best that we're open about it."

And it'd give Weatherly and Shilene time to strategize.

His nerves threatened to get the best of him on the march down the hall. Shilo grabbed his hand. That alone would inform her parents what was going on.

Weatherly and Shilene were in the room, heated words being lobbed back and forth, but the venom wasn't reserved for each other. Frustration with the situation Covet had put them in, fraught anticipation over a physical fight between Ironhorse Falls and Passage Lake, and yes, some speculation on the boundaries crossed by their daughter's bodyguard.

Both looked up when they entered. Waylon closed the door behind them and instead of taking his standard post by the wall, he took a seat next to Shilo.

Shilene didn't miss the change in arrangement. "What's going on?" Her voice held a dangerous edge.

No, this wasn't going to go well. Waylon didn't care, as long as history didn't repeat itself.

"Waylon and I have grown closer." Shilo positioned herself much like Langdon had. "I'm not mating Langdon, and I'm not mating another male to keep me from madness. Waylon is my mate, and he is the only one I will be with."

Langdon's offer went over better than Shilo's announcement.

"No," Weatherly said.

Shilene slammed her hand on the table. "We're not doing this again. I have Langdon Covet pissing on trees like this is his territory and you want to bring up this old argument. We already told you our stance on him. It hasn't changed just because he's your supposed bodyguard."

The level of hostility was as unexpected as it was insulting. But they weren't done with him yet.

"Is he still getting paid?" Weatherly asked. "Do you plan to bond with him and keep him on as bodyguard so he can mooch off our colony supplies like he's done all of his life?"

"What the hell—" Waylon had expected more than resistance, but the personal depth to Weatherly's accusations was unfounded. "I haven't taken a thing from this place." Uncle Wolf had made sure they were self-sufficient and as invisible as possible.

"Father—"

"You're taking Ironhorse Falls' next leader from us." Hatred burned in Weatherly's eyes. "Don't pretend you don't know what she stands to lose. Her job. Her family. You're fine with that?" He probably would've spit if they had been outside. "And you call yourself her mate."

"And why is that?" Shilo spoke the exact words Waylon wanted to ask. "Why would I lose everything because of Waylon? He has done nothing—"

"Exactly," Shilene said. "He's done nothing. He contributes nothing to Ironhorse Falls and has no useful skills."

For a moment of panic, Waylon couldn't think of a single role he'd played in Ironhorse Falls. Arguing with the Ironhorses wasn't going to convince them he and Shilo were right for each other beyond their innate drive to mate.

But there was one thing he did well. "I take care of her." It was the truth.

Weatherly's lip lifted in a sneer. "Our daughter can take care of herself."

"She works for you, she negotiates, she crafts for the colony to keep the various cultures alive. But she doesn't get groceries. She doesn't cook. She doesn't relax and stop doing projects for others. She takes care of others, not herself."

The heartfelt words poured out. He didn't care if he had to don an apron that read *Kiss the Cook*, this was his purpose. He was the yin to Shilo's yang. She was pulled in different directions by her family, her colony, and Covet. He grounded her.

Shilo's hand clasped his. When he looked at her, the love shining in her eyes gave him the first indication that yes, they might make it through this.

"We are meant to be," Shilo said. "He is mine and I am his. He's the reason I could be the strong leader this colony needs and not one who gradually crumbles under the pressure."

Shilene spoke through gritted teeth. "I am not risking what resources we have left to fight the Covet pack only to turn around and give it to another Covet spawn whose own family disposed of him before he could lead their colony."

"Shilene!" Weatherly barked.

"What—" Shilo turned to Shilene.

Waylon's world slowed. Covet spawn? How could that be true? But then, why would they make that claim if they didn't know it was true? They spoke like they knew exactly where he'd come from and how he'd ended up alone in the woods as a little kid.

If the door hadn't been shut already, he would've bolted it closed. Sealed it until he had answers. "Tell me everything you fucking know. Now."

Shilo's chest tightened.

Covet spawn?

Waylon was a Covet?

No. He couldn't be.

For one, he looked nothing like Langdon. Maybe if he chopped his longish hair and styled it in the dapper fashion Langdon favored. They both had cappuccino-colored eyes but there were only so many eye colors in the world. And it wasn't like they both moved their body with enviable confidence, like they were constantly on the prowl and the only reason their prey hadn't been caught yet was because they hadn't chosen to pounce.

"Oh my God" flew out of her mouth. "You're a Covet."

Fear and confusion mingled in his gaze, but she couldn't take it back. Put him in a suit, trim his hair, and have him strut next to Langdon and no shifter in the world would think they weren't related. Slacks so weren't Waylon's style and until the possibility had been proposed, it wasn't an idea that would occur to anyone.

"Everything," Waylon demanded, staring at her parents. "What do you know about my past?"

Weatherly and Shilene didn't have to exchange a look for Waylon to know that they were communicating telepathically. A sizzling string of communication might as well shimmer between them. The hair on Waylon's neck stood just like it had when he'd driven though Passage Lake.

The couple didn't communicate like this often, but Waylon had always been able to tell when. How had he not noticed the actual *sensation* that accompanied it? Chalking it up to body language and expressions, he'd written off his intuition as good observation.

He didn't have time to ponder more, to wonder at all the signs about his abilities he might've missed. Answers about where he came from were within reach, and he wasn't sure he'd like what they were.

"It was a rumor at first," Shilene said, crossing her arms across her chest. "That Passage Lake was afraid you'd survive and challenge Langdon for leadership."

"Why would I do that? I'm not an alpha." Taking the lead wasn't in Waylon's genetics. He saw after himself and those he loved. And the list of those he loved was short.

"You don't have to be to make a family fear it's possible. There was a note with you. It had a name."

More hair twitched along his body. What were Weatherly and Shilene saying to each other?

"Edward C." Shilene said the name like he should know who that was.

"And the C was assumed to be Covet?" Shilo said. "That's a stretch. But it was enough to start a rumor?"

Weatherly cleared his throat. "The Covet pack wasn't always in charge of Passage Lake. That changed around the time we found him."

"Him" was sitting right here. "How did you know what to call me? Why not think Edward was my name?"

"You told us your name was Waylon," Shilene answered. "It was one of the few words you spoke. You were so young, I doubted you remembered much, but you couldn't even tell us your parents' names."

"What did Passage Lake say when you asked them about me?" They had to have checked with the surrounding colonies. Passage Lake was the closest and the only colony Ironhorse Falls had access to. The others were blocked by forest and lakes with no roads connecting them.

"They said you weren't theirs."

Shilene's blunt answer kicked him in the gut. The whole colony had declared him not one of them? What could a child have done to have a whole family turn on him? Unwanted as a kid, unwanted as an adult.

Shilo squeezed his hand. He couldn't look at her. The burn in his chest robbed him of breath. Two colonies had completely rejected him—if Passage Lake was even the home of his origin. A note with Edward C. wasn't proof.

Shilo maintained a firm grip and scooted her chair closer.

Not completely unwanted. The pressure in his chest eased slightly.

He tightened his grip on her strong hand. "So back to Edward C."

"The name traveled the colony, but no one knew an Edward C. One day, Wolf showed up on our doorstep, but he never claimed to know Edward C., only that he'd take you in."

And they'd just handed a toddler over to a stranger no one in town knew? Unbelievable. And fortunate. He'd thrived with Uncle Wolf.

"A Covet? Seriously?" Waylon wasn't able to wrap his mind around the extrapolation. A child no one claimed was related to their arch nemesis.

"Just a rumor that strengthened once you started to get older. The Covets took charge and we interacted with them more often. The resemblance…"

What resemblance? He looked nothing like that arrogant ass. When was the last time he'd worn a suit?

That would be never.

"I see it now," Shilo said.

"What?" No. He was not a Covet. "People can look alike and not be related."

"It's more than looking like him," she said. "It's moving like him. It's brooding like him, only he's so arrogant and you're so…angry." Shilo turned to her mother. "The picture. Do you have a photo of Langdon's parents?"

"No, but I've met them. Long before Langdon was born, we were friendly with all the pack leaders in Covet. Why?"

Waylon pulled out his wallet. The picture hadn't left him since he'd unearthed it. Sliding it across the table, he wanted to withdraw it. Was he the baby in the picture?

Shilene accepted the photo and she and Weatherly studied it.

The buzz of their mind speak charged across Waylon's body. As the expressions on the Ironhorses' faces grew graver and their mind speak went on longer, Waylon reached out.

What do you think they know?

Shilo's hand twitched over his like the interaction had come as a surprise. *I don't know, but I think what they have to say will be enlightening.* She switched to regular talk. "They're familiar then?"

"He is." Weatherly snapped the pic from Shilene and shoved it across the table. "He looks like Langdon's father."

Brothers? Waylon slid the photo toward himself and peered at it. The male did indeed resemble the Covet leader. But why would Uncle Wolf keep this? The people in this picture had meant something to him. Based on their age, and the long life of Uncle Wolf, one of these people had to be Uncle Wolf's kin. Kid? Grandkid? Maybe he'd told Waylon to call him Uncle for a reason. But everyone had called him Uncle.

"But is it Langdon's father?" Shilo asked. "Is this baby Langdon? Or is it Waylon?"

Waylon stuffed the photo back into his wallet, creasing the edge. "Too many damn questions. I need to find the people who know."

Instantly, Weatherly and Shilene's hostility skyrocketed. "You don't need to do anything. You've done enough. No one will be investigating this mystery until we've negotiated with the Covets."

Waylon threw his head back and laughed. "I'm not part of your pack. I'm not even part of your colony, as so many of you have pointed out during my lifetime. Uncle Wolf is dead, I don't answer to you, and this is my life."

Weatherly's face flushed a vibrant red. "We don't need to tolerate you within our perimeter. You're not mating my daughter. You need to leave. Today."

Waylon was going to say something like it wasn't Weatherly's decision, it was Shilo's, but she could stand up for herself.

He waited for her to.

Her hand was limp over his. He chanced a glance, anxiety bubbling in his gut at what emotion he'd find in her eyes. Resolve? Righteous anger? Or the one he feared most: Abandonment?

CHAPTER 15

*S*hilo had a decision to make.

Her colony was in danger. Her future was at risk. And her mate had been told to leave.

Mother spoke to Waylon. "We'll have someone escort you through Passage Lake and watch you to ensure that you don't interfere in colony business. If we catch you so much as saying 'hi' to someone from Passage Lake, or to someone who knows someone from Passage Lake, we'll take action. You know what this means to our colony and you'd be threatening our peace. Your own pack leader couldn't argue our decision."

Maybe it was her lack of a mating bond to stabilize her volatility. Maybe it was the dark future she saw for herself if Waylon left. Or maybe she was just sick of others dictating her life. Her purpose was this colony and she'd lost Waylon to it once already. A mate was the most important part of a shifter's life. Mating and loyalty. Shilo's loyalty had been misplaced the first time around. If her purpose couldn't support her mate, then her loyalty needed to change.

"No need. Waylon and I will leave." The shock in Waylon's

eyes was heartbreaking. He hadn't thought she'd stay by his side, even if he had to leave Ironhorse.

"You can't go," Father sputtered.

She rose, dragging Waylon up with her. "You said I couldn't take over for you if I mated Waylon. I'm mating Waylon, so I'll leave."

Waylon's startled gaze jumped to her.

Mother rose, her eyes wild. This move was the last she'd expected out of her daughter. For the first time in a long time, Shilo's own pride swelled. "Shilo—"

She cut a hand through the air. "No. My decision is made. If I leave, Langdon will no longer have a hold on this place."

"Except to target the next successor we choose," Father said.

"Then you'll have to fight him," she said gravely. "He won't stop. Is that clear now? You were willing to sell me to keep us from fighting. I won't stay with people willing to do that."

Tightening her grip on Waylon's hand, she towed him out of the room.

Where are we going? When Waylon's voice was in her head, all her nerves short-circuited. She had a hard time thinking and not stripping down and demanding to be claimed.

Uncle Wolf's cabin was within the colony perimeter. It wasn't an option. "Your place in West Creek." *Then I think we need to hack Covet's records and find out who you are.*

With what computer genius?

Don't you have connections?

I...maybe.

"Get your backpack. I need to grab some things." She ran upstairs and found her suitcase. Tossing in items that were within reach, she hoped there was enough for a few outfit changes. She'd gone without before, though not because she'd been cut off from all funds.

And family.

Stalling over her suitcase with a fistful of underwear, she blinked back a sudden rush of tears. She'd been packing for a good few minutes and her parents hadn't rushed after her. They either thought her words were empty or they were plotting a way to stop her.

There was still no sign of them as she went to her craft room.

Waylon found her. "What do you need packed?"

She was leaving home for the first time, practically running away like she was sixteen and pissed that she couldn't date who she wanted, yet he didn't berate her for her need to gather her supplies.

Yanking out a few totes she used to transport her products, she shoved beads and folded material inside. She hadn't made it far on Olga's dress, but dammit, she needed to finish it. The importance of the craft dogged her. Olga needed this dress.

Waylon took the totes from her, his own backpack slung over his shoulder. Down the stairs to his Jeep, there was no sign of Mother or Father.

Tiny spikes of tears on the backs of her eyes burned, but she would not cry. She set her suitcase by the hatch of the Jeep and went around to the passenger door. No one rushed out to stop her.

Child or adult, it hurt to feel like her own parents didn't want her.

She was about to open the door but stopped, her hand clasping the handle. Was this only a minute fraction of what Waylon had felt his entire life? As a child alone in the woods, as a boy foisted onto a stranger without question, to the adult who'd had to witness his own mate put him off.

I'm so sorry. Tears streaked down her cheeks.

The hatch slammed shut and he rounded the back.

Rushing to her side, he reached for her and folded her into his warm, strong embrace. "About what?" His words were muffled in her hair.

She looked at her home. The place she'd grown up in and had lived her whole life. No faces peered out the windows; no doors got flung open as frantic parents rushed out.

Waylon followed her gaze, his forehead crinkled.

"They don't care," she whispered.

"They care. Their priorities are shit, but they care. Otherwise, they'd never let you leave with me." He opened the door. She was so numb he had to help her in like a rag doll.

"I shouldn't be in a place where they let me do anything." She should've grown up a long time ago.

"Look." He buckled her in, then leaned in with an arm propped on the open door. "I'm guessing it's a family thing. If there's one thing I learned about being a bartender, it's that family issues are universal despite the species. My customers are adults, but they come in bitching about pushy parents, neglectful parents, parents they can never please. And yes, some of them still live with their parents. You're just setting hard limits."

Only Waylon could've made her feel better about this moment. "Take me home, Waylon."

PASSAGE LAKE WAS in five miles. Shilo peered at the scenery. Even though she was committed to leaving and moving into that warehouse thing with Waylon, she hoped she'd be back. This place was in her blood. It was her home. Had been her home.

Her home was with Waylon now.

"Stop up there." She pointed to a spot where the ditch wasn't steep and the trees weren't thick. A worn portion of the ground jutted off the main road like this was a common meeting point for shifters out running their wolves—or more likely on watchdog duty. Each time she passed it, she'd pondered different reasons for it, but today, she had one use in mind.

"Stop?" Waylon let off the gas. "Is something wrong?"

"No. I want you to claim me on Covet land."

He stomped on the brake. She slammed forward, the belt catching her. Smoothing her hair out of her face after her head whipped back, she pushed down her nerves. Would he do it?

She'd have to show him why he should do it. "Then I want to drive through Passage Lake with your scent all over me and the windows down."

He didn't shut the engine off. "Won't that hurt your parents' strategy planning or whatever?"

"Yes. Langdon's going to find out soon enough and I'm more afraid that if he thinks I'm leaving Ironhorse Falls with you"—which she was—"that he'll try to stop us. What if he blackmails me or somehow forces me to mate him to get Ironhorse Falls? If I'm already claimed, his whole colony will know I wasn't compliant. It'll tarnish his 'but I want the best for you' image."

Waylon didn't answer at first. If he rejected her again, she…deserved it. They'd had several years together, and she'd never asked for his mark despite knowing he'd wanted to officially claim her.

"You really want to do this?" he asked.

"I've always wanted this. Just been too scared."

He looked out her window, then scanned out the Jeep around them. "We'll have to make it fast. I don't want you exposed to them."

"Our kind never used to hide our passion."

He put the Jeep in park. "Yeah, well, that was before

YouTube." His gaze swept down her body and his scent hit her. Hot. Masculine. Turned on. "Get out and pull your pants down."

A surge of lust flooded her system with heat and want and need. Blood rushed to her core and she hopped out. Standing in the open door, her pants had barely passed her butt cheeks when he was behind her, his lips on her neck, his hands over hers, pushing the material down far enough to spread her legs. His big hand skimmed around her waist to dip down and cup her sex.

"I'm ready." She ground her ass into him. The coarse material of his pants and the scratch of his zipper were delicious sensations on her needy flesh.

"I want to be sure." His breath wafted over her neck, sending shivers down her flushed body. One finger pushed through her sex, swiping her clit.

As good as it felt, this was taking too damn long. She wanted this male. He was hers and she wanted the world to know they belonged to each other. No wonder humans wore wedding rings. She'd wear a tiara at this point to get the word out. For too long she'd held back, overly aware of what others thought of her.

"I want you to fuck me hard. Right now." She reached behind her to fumble with the button and zipper of his pants. He didn't help, but stroked along her folds, then dabbed at her clit, switching between them over and over again. She needed several attempts to open his trousers. She kept bucking and arching into his touch and losing her grip.

Finally, she freed him.

He took over, freeing her hands to anchor herself on the cool metal of the vehicle as he thrust inside.

Waylon did just what he'd said they had to do. He made it fast. She tipped her head to the side and pulled her sleeve down to make room for his mouth. As soon as his fangs punctured her neck, she came hard and wet against his hand. Her fingers dug into the frame of the Jeep. They'd fucked like this before, but this time it was more than just a position. It was the call of their wolves to embed their scents into their mates, to warn off other prospective lovers, to repel them.

Their scents mingled. His with hers. Hers with his. Any shifter who came across them, whether she and Waylon were apart or together, would know they belonged to each other.

A full mating ceremony was next, but she wanted to settle in with Waylon first.

"God, baby. That was amazing." He was still inside of her. His feet were braced and his arms around her, his hand at her center but holding her gently.

Peeling her hands off the frame of the Jeep, she straightened. He slipped out and helped her get her leggings up before stuffing his magnificence back into his own pants.

"That was the most amazing." She sucked in a lungful of pine- and earth-scented air. Centered. Balanced. When was the last time she'd experienced this level of tranquility?

Why had she waited so long? What would it be like when they finally bonded?

Complete. That's how she'd feel.

She spun around and palmed his face with both hands. "I'm sorry I made us wait so long."

He yanked her to him for a quick kiss. "It's done now. No more apologies from either of us. You're mine, and we'll make it permanent as soon as we can."

"It is permanent." She stared down the road. "Now let's go piss off Langdon Covet."

"SHOULD I CRACK THE WINDOW?" Waylon glared down the road.

"Absolutely."

He did more than crack it. The window went all the way down, wind blowing through the cab. He'd been through Passage Lake enough to know that the gas station on this edge of town was Langdon's perch for monitoring the comings and goings of his people and those from Ironhorse Falls. The stations on both sides of town were just security gates disguised as normal businesses. Waylon bet this place had a tiny convenience store and a palatial office with opulence that didn't fit the exterior.

Shilo pressed her hands into her thighs, her gaze not missing any details.

Waylon slowed to the speed limit. As they passed the building, Langdon came into view. He leaned against the entrance of the station. His suit coat was off, his starched white shirt had the sleeves rolled up, and the first two buttons were undone.

Waylon slid his gaze away but kept his eye on the rearview mirror. Shilo didn't smile, nod, or wave. She didn't so much as tip her head.

Langdon pushed off the wall. Even as he faded in the rearview mirror, the rage in his features was clear. The Jeep stuttered, but the engine didn't quit.

A black SUV was parked to his right at the sole stoplight in town. Both front doors opened and the two from the meeting got out. They couldn't have arrived much earlier than him and Shilo.

But they didn't stop him. Were they the shifters who patrolled the woods and stalled vehicles in order to dig into others' business?

The other gas station was coming up. Paulie was dressed the same. He hadn't had time to get out of his coveralls.

Shilo's voice entered his thoughts. *Think we should stop and ask if you're going to get invited to the next family reunion? Too soon?*

A laugh burst out of Waylon. Fierce suspicion in Paulie's eyes flared like his nostrils.

Shilo giggled. Like they'd planned it, they both gave Paulie a salute as they passed.

"I should feel guilty about the trouble that's going to cause Mother and Father."

"Covet was going to cause trouble anyway."

"True."

Neither one could fully relax until they were out of Covet territory.

He rolled his window back up. It was time to take Shilo home.

If only *his* home felt right.

CHAPTER 16

With the fabric stretched over the counter, Shilo was able to move around and cut out the pattern. She hadn't bought a cheapo sewing machine yet. She should've brought hers along, but she hadn't been thinking clearly.

Waylon had sensed an impending panic attack when she realized she'd forgotten it and reassured her that he could afford a new machine since hers was currently six hours away.

Shilo jolted. She'd been stalled mid cut, thinking about the last week she'd been in Freemont.

Her parents hadn't contacted her.

"Maybe they don't have a cell signal." Waylon came up behind her, rested one hand on her hip, and grabbed the scissors from her hand with the other.

"I'm not think—" Why was she bothering to deny it? This was Waylon. Only they'd switched roles.

He was the one working and she was the one without a job. So she needed to take care of him, and it was getting late. He was dressed in a black tee that hugged his sculpted chest like she did each night they went to bed together. The blue jeans on his long legs only made him look rugged and approachable.

And he got approached. Every shift. She smelled it on him. Lust. One-way horniness that he brushed off and didn't give a second thought to beyond his "no."

Shilo had instinctively stayed away from Pale Moonlight. Sitting at the edge of the bar, growling at every female who ordered a drink or even smiled at Waylon wasn't good for her or Pale Moonlight.

Waylon turned her into his embrace and dropped a kiss on her mouth. "Need anything before I get home?"

"No." She hadn't left the loft. Waylon got the groceries and dammit, he even had to cook them. She'd been watching cooking shows but she hated the chore and they both liked Waylon's food better.

"You can call a cab or Uber or something and get the machine tonight." He'd offered last night. And the night before. He was starting to get worried about her.

"We'll see how I feel." Which was to not go anywhere. Her hair was in a messy bun and she was wearing an old pair of his basketball shorts and a tattered T-shirt he'd meant to convert to rags. Her packing job had been subpar and she couldn't blow money she wasn't earning for a new wardrobe. "I think I'll call Armana though. See what she found out."

Except for the sewing machine money, Waylon was saving the cash he'd earned for Armana and the researcher-slash-hacker she'd yet to find. She understood how critical discretion was, but it wasn't easy to find a shifter who could dig that potentially deep and remain undetected.

Waylon nodded but didn't move away. "Everything okay?"

How could it be all right? "I'm with you. That's all that matters now."

He set a wad of cash down on the counter next to the

dress material. "Last night was good for tips. Bachelorette party. We moved them out pretty quick and managed to keep the tipsy bride-to-be out of the back rooms."

Shilo made herself laugh. "Humans."

Waylon wasn't fooled. "Seriously, Shilo. Are you okay?"

"It's a transition. To be expected." Only it was nothing like Shilo had expected. She had Waylon back. She was mentally stable, enough that she could hang with Waylon for years and keep her feral instincts at bay. It was like the madness had never happened.

He kissed her again. She curved into him. This part she craved, the feeling of being wanted. Ironically, it helped her forget to think about Waylon and how he'd lived under worse duress his entire life than she had for one week.

"I love you," she murmured against his lips.

"You're my everything. I don't care who I am as long I'm with you."

She smiled and gazed into his eyes. "When'd you get so soft? Go to work and beat those females off you with a stick."

He flashed a smile with a hint of fang. The spot he had marked tingled. "It's better since I have your scent all over me."

She would put her scent all over him again, but he couldn't be late. "Have a good night. I'll be fine. Promise."

One last kiss and he was out the door. She was alone again.

She picked up the scissors again. Staring at the half-cut fabric, her thoughts touched on the same topic they did every night Waylon left for work.

This was Waylon's life. For five years, she'd been steeped in jealously about how easily he'd moved on, but all he did was sleep, eat, work out, and go to work. Like her, he had filled his time with pointless distractions that had moved on as soon as the climax faded.

Five years lost, all to make a point. Her job was important, but not more important than him.

But with no role in the colony, she was stuck with the *now whats*.

Shifting her grip on the scissors, she bent over her work. First, Olga's dress. She'd get it cut out while waiting for Armana's call.

Time flew by as she lost herself in the calming work of crafting. Her happy spot. All the pieces were cut. She was folding the main dress section when suspicion wormed its way in.

Can I trust Waylon?

The material hung limp in her hands.

He gets hit on so much, does he reject them all? We've only been reunited for a few weeks.

Shaking her head, she finished her task and laid all the items on the edge of the counter.

All those scents he comes home with.

Dammit! Where were these worries coming from? This was Waylon. Besides, she was a shifter. She'd know.

To concentrate on a more comfortable duty, she gave up waiting and called Armana.

"Ms. Ironhorse. I was just about to ring."

Shilo smiled. Armana's no-nonsense tone reminded her of home. From what she knew, the female had once helped her first mate lead their colony before he was killed. Now mated to a human and running her own business with him, Armana was one of the most chill shifters Shilo had ever met. Had Mother ever dreamed of leaving the constant stress of colony leadership behind and just living life on her own terms?

Mother and Father were a team, but the last decade had taken its toll. Covet had only added a metric ton of stress to their lives.

Was that why they were so intent on grooming her for the role?

Armana jumped right in without Shilo having to ask. "I've located a computer specialist, and she's willing to dig up any records without me having to go into detail about why."

"I'd have to ask why she doesn't care about the whys."

Armana chuckled, not insulted at all. "Me, too. All I had to say was that we suspect a colony of hoarding technological advances to oppress their people and others and she was so indignant I could barely talk her into limiting her search to the Covet bloodline. I can give you her price quotes if your mother is interested."

"I can pass it on." Would Mother listen? Would the computer specialist—hacker—be put in danger? "When will she have some files to share?"

"Give her a couple of days. She's setting up a secure account and I can get the log-in credentials to you, but we'll wait until you need to use it."

"Right. Keep it as secure as possible. Oh, I have a photo in case it'll help with her search at all."

"Once you log in, upload it."

"Thanks, Armana." Hanging up with Armana, she was filled with excitement. The emotion withered under the constant thread of worry.

Can I trust Waylon?

Is he true?

Maybe he's bitter about what happened between us. What if he holds a grudge?

Is he using me?

She snarled and tossed the phone onto the counter. Putting her hands to her temples, she wandered around the apartment.

Stop it. Just stop it.

Where was this crazy coming from? She was finally

feeling whole again, strong enough to take on the obstacles lobbed her way. Major ones, like her family letting her leave. She was saner than she had been in years, and yet…

Bumping into the punching bag, she opened her eyes.

Waylon's gloves rested on the weight bench to her right. She put them on and found the tape.

Waylon worked for another seven hours. She'd beat the shit of this bag and by the time she was done, maybe she'd be too tired to worry about the male she loved.

WAYLON WAS STARTING to worry about Shilo. The last three nights, he'd gotten home to a Shilo so sweaty, so worn, that she hardly managed a shower before collapsing into bed.

Before he left for work in the evening, she basically attacked him.

He wouldn't complain. Rough sex was good sex when it was with Shilo, but the frantic motivation behind it disturbed him. He'd tried for slow and sweet this morning and tears had shimmered in her eyes. So he'd taken her like a maniac and told her he loved her at least four times before he left for work.

"Hey, Christian. Can I take off a couple hours early? I got a thing with Shilo." Waylon scrubbed a glass with a clean towel to keep his hands busy. He never asked to leave early, and he didn't have a good reason why.

"Sure, man. Whatever you need." Just when Waylon thought he was getting away with no questions, Christian nailed him with a knowing stare. "Everything okay?"

A quick yes was on the tip of his tongue, but Christian would smell the bullshit in his answer. "I don't know. Shilo's been acting…different."

"Family troubles?"

"Maybe. It seems deeper. More personal." How could it get more personal than her parents? But that was how Waylon interpreted it.

"Someone messing with her?"

Waylon put the glass down. "She talks to Armana and that's it." He hadn't detailed the mystery of his birth, but Christian wasn't a nosy leader.

Christian dropped his voice to barely audible. "Shifters are crafty bastards. Someone's been dicking with your life. They could be doing the same to her." How the fuck had Christian known? The male nodded like Waylon had asked the question out loud. "It was clear as a bell, between what the Ironhorses said about you and what I saw for myself. You're not wanted in Ironhorse Falls and as soon as you find out why, or by who, then I think your life will change. Get on home now."

Waylon didn't waste time. He could ponder Christian's insights on his way home.

He dove into his Jeep and managed to keep from squealing out of the parking lot. A few blocks from home, he pulled up behind a mechanic shop and parked. He needed to think. Once he walked into his apartment, he'd have Shilo's troubles to handle.

If someone was getting to Shilo, how would they do it? She hadn't mentioned talking to anyone other than Armana.

Covet shifters had already demonstrated potent mental abilities. If they were in the vicinity and targeting Shilo, he'd feel them.

Waylon slipped out of his Jeep and jogged toward his apartment, keeping to the shadows and stopping frequently to use his senses.

The closer he got to his home, the more the hairs at the back of his neck stood on end.

Someone was nearby using their abilities. He knew it in his bones.

After all these years, he had something to contribute other than a steady hand to fill lip balm containers. He was like a Geiger counter for shifter abilities.

He changed course to pad down the alley that'd give him glimpses of the roads that ran on each side of his place. The avenue behind the row of offices was his concern. Shifters targeting Shilo wouldn't do it from the road in front of his place.

Grateful he was in another black T-shirt, he crouched and sped down the alley. Each gap between the buildings, he peeked out.

There. A car with two people.

Waylon narrowed his eyes. A male and a female. Their shadows resembled the two who were always with Langdon. Oscar and Brynley.

Fuckers.

His body was tingling, little zings of electricity running up and down his nerve pathways.

He had to check on Shilo.

Backtracking, he crossed the alley and went to the street in front of his place. The few cars and pickups parked along the curb and in the lots were empty. The shifters didn't want to be seen. More and more suspicious. He'd chosen this part of town based on availability, cost, and the lack of shifters around, the least hostile environment he'd ever known. He darted in and out of shadows until he got to his front door.

He let himself in and charged up the stairs. Bursting through the door, he squatted down and put his hand to his lips.

Shilo spun away from the bag she was wailing on. Rivulets of sweat ran down her face, over her shoulders, trailing down her back.

Holy shit. Did she beat the bag the entire time he was gone?

The most disturbing part was the anguish in her eyes. Relief flashed in their brown depths, but was brief. Her sides heaved and her gaze traveled to the empty water bottle that had been abandoned on the floor. She licked her lips like she was parched and scowled at him.

He scanned the room. Vibrations sped up and down his spine.

He spoke only loud enough for her to hear. "Someone's targeting you, using telepathy or empathy or some shit, but they're fucking with you."

She blinked and wiped off her face with the back of her hand. "What are you talking about?"

"I can feel them."

He waited a second and her breathing slowed. She looked less ravaged and more confused. "Are you sure?"

"My ability is stronger when I'm with you, and growing more precise. I get twitchy when a shifter is using a mental power around me, and before I got in here, I wanted to vibrate off the sidewalk. Think about it. Do your feelings make sense?"

She glared toward the window, and the storm in her eyes calmed.

"It's not me," she breathed. Her body folded until her butt hit the floor. She heaved a mighty sigh and collapsed back, her arms sprawled to the side and her eyes closed.

He rushed to her side, but she was more relaxed than she'd been in days.

"It's not me," she said again, opening her eyes, her smile dreamy. "Oh my God, it's not you either."

"Me?"

Rage tightened her expression. "Those fuckers." She sat up and peeled the boxing gloves off.

Waylon rested on his heels. "What's been going on?"

Tossing the gloves aside, she prodded her temples. "I thought I was going crazy again. Three nights ago I started getting hit with these major insecurities. Did you really love me? Could you be faithful? Why would you want to?"

"And you used the bag to get through it? Why not talk to me?"

She dropped her hands and gazed at him. "Because I felt stupid. We've reunited, you've been working every night to keep the money coming in, and here I was with debilitating anxiety about what a good male you are. I *know* you are. Questioning it felt...traitorous."

He wrapped her in his arms. "You fought it. You didn't know those thoughts weren't coming from your own mind, yet you still fought them."

"I think you might need a new bag."

He chuckled and looked up at the red punching bag. It'd been used when he bought it, and Shilo was right. A few more nights of this treatment, and all the stuffing would drain out, or a rafter would drop the swinging load.

"I think I saw them." Waylon pointed to where the car would be sitting. "Do you still feel them?"

"I will rip them apart," she growled. Then she shook her head. "Those thoughts are still bombarding me. But it's easier now to tell they're foreign and not from me."

She went to rise, but he tugged her into his lap. Resting her sweaty head against his, she paused for a moment, then jerked her eyes up. "Do you think they made me think I was going rogue?"

"At the least, I think their interference would worsen what was already happening."

She laughed, the sound full of scorn. "I don't know whether I ought to thank them or murder them. If I hadn't been going so crazy so quickly, I wouldn't have leaned on you until I came to my senses."

She grinned. The strain hadn't left her eyes. He knew what she meant, but those Covets had to be taken care of. He could call the local Guardians, but the shifters weren't breaking any laws of their kind, nor were they risking exposure. It was up to him and Shilo.

Waylon grabbed Shilo's hand. "Let's go."

He took the same path to return to the spot in the alley where he could show Shilo the car.

She glared at the vehicle. *I say we go full wolf and scratch the shit out of their car.*

They'd try to turn us into road hash. Are you still feeling their influence?

It's better out here. Like they're targeting the apartment.

That's a hell of an ability. He tried not to be jealous.

So is yours. It creates a safe zone, and I bet several pack leaders would hate to have you at meetings. She couldn't hide her sadness. She would've been one of those pack leaders. But here they were, in a dark alley.

He evaluated their position. *I don't think one of us can get on the other side of them without being seen.*

Open approach. Better than nothing.

Enough to scare them away. There was no way to shield Shilo from their gifts, or they could use this knowledge to their advantage. Instead, the Covets needed to be stopped.

He went first, swaggering to the best of his ability, a cocky grin on his face. "Look who we have here."

"Oscar and Brynley Covet. Brother and sister extraordinaire," Shilo taunted. The two shifters couldn't deny their identity now. And the shock and alarm crossing both their faces were priceless.

The window of the black sedan rolled down. "What the fuck do you two want?"

"To know why you're parked outside of Waylon's place in the middle of the night," Shilo said.

"Pack business," Oscar said, rolling the window back up.

Waylon reached the car and gripped the edge of the window. The motor whirred, but he wouldn't allow it to rise. "Here's the thing." As he spoke, Shilo sauntered in front of the car to the passenger side. She looked like they'd had an extra-sweaty session in bed and was irritated it'd gotten interrupted. "Some asshole shifter is in the area, using their abilities on my mate. What a coincidence, two assholes are parked on the street."

Oscar's lips curled, but Brynley smiled sweetly. "What a coincidence. I'm *looking* at two assholes on the street."

Waylon lifted his hand. "Solid burn, bro."

She sneered like her brother.

Shilo folded her arms across her chest. "I'll make sure to mention to my parents that we happened to see you nearby."

Brynley's expression turned saccharine again. "You do that. For some reason, Ironhorse Falls doesn't seem all that worried you left."

Was it Waylon's imagination, or did Oscar send his sister a warning glare?

Waylon straightened. If Covet had shifters roaming the woods and breaking down vehicles with their minds, what was to stop them from influencing members of any colony they wanted?

What was to stop them from turning the whole town against Shilo?

Icicles chilled his blood.

What was to stop them from turning the whole town against *him*? He eyed the other two shifters more critically. There was something else wrong, other than their lying faces, and he couldn't pinpoint it. The street looked the same as it always did. Smelled the same. But something was different besides the shifter twins parked on the curb.

"Go on any nice runs around Ironhorse Falls lately?" Waylon asked.

Shilo cast a speculative look at him over the top of the car, but she didn't say anything. Her nostrils flared. She sensed something was off. Between them, maybe they could pinpoint the oddity with their unwanted not-quite guests.

Oscar sniffed like it was a stupid question. "I'm a shifter. You've been among humans too long if you even have to ask that."

Shilo snorted. "Bet you end up with a human."

Brynley scoffed. "We'd never mate a human."

"You'd better hope not. I'm sure any mate has to be cleared by your dear cousin," Shilo said. "And I'm sure he'd hate for the Covet bloodline to be diluted by humans."

Brynley's furtive glance at her brother didn't go unnoticed. And the quickly hidden alarm in Oscar's eyes intrigued Waylon.

"Let me guess," Waylon said, "you either have a human mate and keep her secret, or you fear having a mate at all and what your maniacal, calculating cousin will do."

"Fuck you and your assumptions, Wolf." Oscar started the car. "You wouldn't know what being part of a pack is like."

"I obviously know what it's like to have not only a pack, but an entire colony shun me," Waylon replied.

Shilo added, "And I know what it's like to have to leave because of my mate. Keep that in mind next time you throw yourselves behind your ruthless leader."

"He's family," Brynley said much less adamantly than she'd probably intended. "You're an Ironhorse. 'Nuff said."

Both windows rolled up and Oscar drove off.

Waylon stayed on the street and watched them go. "Think

those fuckers convinced the town to hate me? Or are we giving them too much power?"

"Insidious thoughts stretched over many years? That wouldn't drain them too badly."

Made sense. "Building on suspicion that was already there."

"Assholes."

Waylon nodded. "Assholes that seem to fear Langdon Covet."

They could use that.

CHAPTER 17

*S*hilo tapped her leg against the counter. Waylon would be home from work soon. Armana had swung by and dropped a laptop off. Brand new. Only one file with several documents downloaded. And a warning from Armana. *The specialist said someone, or someones, worked very hard to erase Waylon's existence. She didn't find much, but maybe it'll lead you to answers.*

She was jittery, like the computer would self-destruct in T minus five seconds if she waited any longer.

Waylon came through the door, the cloying scent of arousal, sweat, and alcohol riding the wave inside. Only since they'd confronted Oscar and Brynley three days ago, Shilo wasn't a ragey, exhausted bag of female.

But she still hit the bag to keep the stress down.

"Just the male I was waiting for," she said and flipped open the top. She hadn't so much as looked at the on button, afraid she couldn't stop her curiosity from just doing one more thing until *boom*, she was combing through all the info that was pertinent to her mate.

He grinned, the hint of fang reminding her body of all the

167

biting from the previous day. "I hope I'm the only male you're waiting for."

Wiggling in her seat to ease the sudden ache, she turned on the computer. Later. This was important. "Armana said there wasn't much."

Waylon's gaze lit on the bright boot-up screen. "She found something?"

"Not as much as we hoped. But I think from the lack of information she found, we can deduce that you have something to do with the Covets and they'd don't like it. Your history's been wiped."

Hope lowered to a simmer in his eyes. "Let's see what she found."

Only two documents were in the file, but there were five photos.

Waylon scooted a stool closer to her and sat. "What's with all the pictures?"

"Armana scanned the photo we found and passed the image along to the specialist. She might've found similar ones." Shilo hovered the cursor over the files. "You pick. Which one first?"

Waylon took her hand off the tracking pad and folded it into his. His warmth surrounded her from that little contact. "I need you to know that whatever we find, I'm still Waylon Wolf."

Why the hesitation? She'd clocked down the minutes until he returned, her mind spinning over what they might find. To her, it wouldn't change anything.

But not to Waylon. She realized that now. He'd had to form his own identity. There'd been no pack to guide him. Uncle Wolf had taught him to survive, but Waylon had figured himself out. And he might have to make the journey again after she opened the file.

She squeezed his fingers. "It's not a fork in the road where I go one way and you go the other. We stay together."

"Okay. Documents first."

Shilo opened the one the specialist had simply titled *1*. The other file was labeled *Hard to Find*.

They simultaneously leaned into the screen.

A birth certificate? Shilo scanned the information. It was for Langdon's father.

"Is there anything here you didn't know?" Waylon asked.

"I didn't know his parents' names. Layton and Orina Covet. Layton took over the colony shortly after Langdon was born. Mother said it was a contentious fight that much of the colony didn't agree with."

Waylon pointed to one box. "Langdon's not that much younger than me."

But they didn't know Waylon's exact birthday.

Shilo clicked open the Hard to Find document. "Another birth certificate?"

"Mine?" The hopefulness in his voice was clear.

She scrolled down. "Two boys. Layton and Payton Covet. Same birthdate, but Payton is three minutes older." Langdon's dad had a twin. Shilo couldn't see the significance.

"Holy shit, look at the parents' names."

Shilo's jaw dropped. "Edward and Kayleen Covet. *Edward C.*, from the note? Maybe the note wasn't *your* name, it was the intended recipient's name. And that's why Uncle Wolf took you in once he heard about the note. At least, that's what Mother was alluding to, I think."

"I was raised by Langdon's grandfather? I doubt it." Waylon huffed out a breath. He stared at the document for another minute and shook his head. "The only birth certificate I care about is mine. I dunno. Maybe the hacker thought we could find a worthy opponent to challenge Langdon for the colony?"

Shilo shrugged and tapped on a photo. She and Waylon squinted at it. Not a photo, but more like a microfiche snapshot from an old newspaper. The article next to it had little detail other than that the photo had been taken at a harvest parade.

"That looks like the guy from your picture," she said. She didn't have to point to the guy on the horse in between two floats.

Waylon nodded, frustration shimmering in his eyes. "How about the next one?"

Another one from the parade, a broader view of the lineup, but this photo hijacked their full attention.

Shilo said what they were both thinking. "The guy in Uncle Wolf's picture was either Langdon's dad or his twin."

The article was the same as the last. Harvest parade, blah, blah, blah. What was the third picture? She opened it to find a smiling man holding two squirmy bundles. Another microfiche that had been digitally uploaded. Shilo's mouth curved up. Langdon's greed for technology had worked against him. The headline of the article read: *Edward Covet cradles the future of Covet pack, disappears years later.*

"I'll be damned," Shilo said. "That's Uncle Wolf. He really was Edward Covet."

"No." Waylon's denial was resolute, but his expression scrunched. "I would know if I was raised by a Covet."

"It's not like they were a thorn in Ironhorse Falls' side until Langdon took power."

"Then why'd Uncle Wolf leave? What happened to him?"

Waylon knew Uncle Wolf better than anyone, but how could one male age so drastically in a few decades? In the picture, the father of the twins wore a broad smile with pitch-black hair. He was hearty and filled out with muscle, not haggard and world worn, with gray hair and a ragged beard.

"It's hard to believe, but after the last month..." He tapped the screen. "Look at him. I never saw him smile."

Each picture was more and more interesting. The fourth picture contained no actual photos, just a lone article. Shilo read through it, her shock rising with each sentence.

Uncle Wolf—Edward Covet—had lost his mate, a son, his son's mate, and a grandbaby in a fire. Edward was a person of suspicion but hadn't been found since his disappearance thirty years prior.

She exchanged a look with Waylon. No wonder Uncle Wolf had been an aged shell of himself. He'd lost his entire family. Except for his surviving son, Layton.

"Uncle Wolf didn't kill them." Waylon spoke with confidence. "He wasn't that type of male."

It didn't make sense. "Why would Uncle Wolf turn away from Layton during his darkest time?"

"He lost his mate. He might not have known what he was doing. Did you see the date? It's before Covet took over the colony."

Shilo chewed on her lip. She'd been raised under colony politics. There was a glaring problem with this scenario.

"So... Uncle Wolf was presumably the pack leader for Covet, who used to be a subservient pack in Passage Lake. The son that would take over for him is tragically killed in a fire, along with his heir, and boom, Layton Covet, Langdon's dad, challenges and wins leadership over the colony. And all this happens around the time you were found wandering on Ironhorse Falls land."

"Suspicious as fuck."

"Yep. But say you were Payton's son and Uncle Wolf's grandson. Layton won the challenge fair and square. His rule is undisputed until he is mysteriously killed years later. Langdon was too little to have anything to do with the family murders. He wasn't to blame and would stay leader."

"My only threat to him would be that I could challenge him for the role, which I'm seriously not interested in. But that doesn't make me any different than any other ambitious Passage Lake member."

One more picture. Waylon reached across her to click it open. Layton's obituary.

Waylon leaned back and shoved both hands in his hair. "He died the same time I found Uncle Wolf dead in front of the cabin."

"This is some straight-up soap opera shit going on. What do we do with the info?" she asked. Waylon might have a claim to the Covet pack, but he was the last person who wanted the position. He'd never wanted to lead. He hung back, watched over others, listened for the real problem.

"Oscar's a weak point. We spy on him, then blackmail him to bring us one of the Covet pack members who was there when Layton took over."

Whoa. That was…way more hardcore than her previous role as negotiator. It was also more than cowering in his apartment, beading a garment that, while a work of art, wasn't going to save her colony from Langdon Covet.

But it was what the future leader of Ironhorse Falls would do to save her people. Langdon had proved the lengths he'd go to protect himself. He used subversive tactics and she knew outright force was only his last choice, not his last option.

"If Oscar's coming to Freemont to see a human mate, we can nab him in town."

"I say we need to stalk that waitress he was flirting with from the night at the restaurant." He gave her a grin. "Chinese for lunch?"

~

"This is really boring."

Waylon smiled at Shilo's impatience. She wouldn't have survived a cabin in the woods with no TV, no projects, and nothing to do but hunt and gather. Admittedly, this was worse. They were in his Jeep, with limited legroom, parked a block away from their surveillance target in the lot of a burger joint.

She balled up a fast-food bag and tossed it into the backseat. The last two hamburgers were on her lap. She handed one over. "We can't even go inside and eat real food. Their kung pao chicken is awesome."

Unwrapping a burger, she scowled at the thin patty.

Waylon chuckled and took a bite out of his, leaving only half of it behind. No, it wasn't kung pao chicken, but it filled him.

He finished his mouthful and said, "You're just spoiled from my cooking."

"Can't deny it."

Day four of watching the Chinese restaurant and the sense of anticipation churning in his gut might just be indigestion. When the restaurant was open, they spied on it. It was too risky to have Shilo out by herself. Between the two of them, they could watch each other's backs. The two nights he'd had off, they'd driven to the edge of Freemont, shifted, and watched the highway coming from Passage Lake.

Nothing.

Shilo's restlessness was spilling over to him. He had to keep telling himself—and her—that they had time. Not much before Ironhorse Falls either fought or fell, but with only the two of them, they couldn't march into Passage Lake and demand to talk to all the older families.

Shilo slapped his arm. "There she is again."

Waylon tossed his own wrapper in the back and peered at the restaurant. It was after the lunch rush, and the leggy blonde who'd flirted with Oscar the night Waylon had finally been with Shilo again strutted into the restaurant.

She'd worked last night, but no luck on the Oscar front. Why wasn't he willing to fight for his mate? Langdon might force him to mate another, since that seemed to be his thing.

A man followed the woman to the door, holding it open for her, but when she disappeared inside, he let the door shut and remained outside. His hands were shoved in his pockets and he looked around the parking lot—not casually, but with intent.

"Isn't that the bartender from the night we met Langdon here?" Shilo asked. "I had wondered if Oscar knew him, the way the guy couldn't take his eyes off Oscar."

Waylon defaulted to the game they'd started to fend off the boredom. "He's a secret agent."

She rolled her eyes. "You always start with that. Student. Young, but maybe not undergrad young. Masters?"

"That's ageist. He could've been in the army, gone to Afghanistan, now he's finishing school and working here part-time."

"Or maybe he did hard time, is trying to turn away from a life of selling drugs and works three jobs to pay the rent."

Waylon nodded and twisted to clean up the back. He bunched wrappers into a pile for easy cleanup. It was looking like another boring day. He might have to recline the seat back and get some more shuteye since he'd worked last night. "The rent part might be true. If Christian didn't pay so well, I would've been hitting the streets, putting applications in all over town for a second job."

Shilo leaned forward, an odd tone in her voice. "Or he's the real reason Oscar won't tell Langdon about his mate."

Waylon turned around. What was she talking about?

His eyes widened. A familiar black sedan had pulled up to the backdoor and the bartender slid into the passenger seat.

Waylon looked up in time to see him meet Oscar over the console for a kiss.

Not just any kiss. An I-missed-you-down-to-my-soul kiss. Like the one Waylon had finally been able to give Shilo at Uncle Wolf's cabin.

"That's his human mate," Shilo breathed. "And he hasn't told Langdon."

"I bet his sister covers for him when they come to Freemont and West Creek to do Langdon's bidding."

"But why the secrecy? The human part, or the man part?"

Waylon pondered the couple. They were embracing and kissing and murmuring to each other. Langdon had his priorities and the main one was to limit competition. Human mates posed little competition, other than a cheering squad for the mate who might oppose Langdon, but Langdon was the type to think they made a colony weak.

Was that why Oscar was hiding this guy?

Waylon opened his door. "I say we go ask him."

~

THE MYSTERY of Oscar's relationship propelled Shilo forward. The whys weren't as important as much as how they could use the information to make Oscar help them.

Making a wide circle, she approached the car from behind while Waylon took the front. She'd asked why she couldn't approach and relish the shock on Oscar's face, but Waylon didn't want him to gun the vehicle and mow her down.

Fair enough. But now she had to worry about Waylon becoming a hood ornament.

She'd just cleared the parking lot behind Oscar and his boyfriend when Waylon jogged up to them, waving.

His mouth was stretched in a shit-eating grin. "Oscar, buddy. I thought that was you. Who's your friend?"

From this angle, she could see Oscar's head snap up as the taillights flared. The bartender flattened himself against the passenger seat. Oscar jerked his gaze to the rearview mirror, his reverse lights dim in the bright sun. He saw her and slammed the car into park.

His curse was audible through the closed windows as he slumped into his seat.

Waylon made the motion to roll down his window. Same as the other night, she went to the passenger seat.

The bartender didn't meet her eyes and his window stayed up. She inhaled, trying to scent him, but he was strangely blank. She hadn't paid him much attention the night she'd been drinking in the bar.

Waylon's voice floated through her head. *Did you feel like something was off when we confronted Oscar and Brynley?*

Yes. She'd chalked it up to the situation at the time. She'd been too consumed with roiling emotions toward Waylon, thanks to the twins' mental push.

But she understood what he'd meant. Something was off.

Waylon leaned down, the same overly friendly grin on his face. "I'm Waylon Wolf. You are?"

"None of your business," Oscar growled.

The man's head stayed bent as he stared at the floor. His anxiety wafted over her. Funny how that was the first scent she'd really associated with him—

"That's it," she said, hitting the top of the car one time. Three heads spun her away. "No scent. Brynley's the empath. You're a scent scrubber."

Oscar went rigid. No wonder they were indispensable to Langdon. He could use Brynley to influence others' thinking, and with Oscar along, no one would know another shifter had been in the area.

Waylon gave her a look over the hood that said *wouldn't I know*? He should sense Oscar using his ability. She lifted a shoulder. The effect might have a long half-life. She'd spent the day emotionally exhausted, with lingering jealousy, long after the twins had probably gone home.

Waylon bent to look Oscar in the eye. "Let me smell your boy there."

"Fuck off, pervert."

Shilo would feel guilty if it weren't for all the shit Oscar had put her through. "I guess we'll have to ask Langdon why you'd hide your boyfriend from him."

Oscar's terrified gaze met hers. "You'd get Jason killed," he hissed.

"Oscar." Jason gave up his restraint and reached for Oscar. They clung hands.

Okay, guilt seeped into Shilo. She had a grudge against Oscar, not his innocent mate, but they had to get to the bottom of this.

"Jason obviously knows about our kind. So why are you hiding him from Langdon?" Shilo asked.

Oscar briefly squeezed his eyes closed, like what he had to say was going to make him sick. "You already guessed why. Diluting the family's powers isn't in Langdon's grand plan, but creating pairings to optimize abilities is. He'd dismiss Jason and find a female for me to mate and reproduce with." Oscar's flinty eyes sparked. "And expect me to be okay watching Jason die a normal human death. Langdon takes after his old man. That bastard didn't respect his mate or anyone else's." Oscar glanced at Waylon. "They're pawns in his game."

Anger burned through her. From what she'd learned about Langdon, this sounded exactly like him. "Being my mate isn't his only issue with Waylon. Why?"

Oscar glanced at Waylon and dropped his gaze to the

steering wheel. "He's our long lost cousin, I guess. Langdon said Waylon's father was a traitor and that Waylon would be, too."

"And you bought that?" Shilo put all of her scorn into her question. Something smelled off, but if Oscar was lying, he could hide it.

"I went along with it," Oscar said. "There's a difference."

"Why?" Waylon asked. His humor had faded and his tone had softened. She couldn't imagine the betrayal he must be experiencing. This male was his kin.

"Bad shit happens around Langdon's relatives and it only improves his place in the colony. I could argue, I could leave, but then I'd end up dead. Loose ends get clipped. I've heard him say it."

"Okay, *cousin*," Waylon bit out. "Why did Langdon's dad kill mine? Why am I still alive?"

"I was just a kid. Pack politics? Spite? The guy got a kick out of screwing people. As for why you're still alive, I dunno. Your parents were able to get you out."

Shilo shook her head. Wrong answer. "You're going to have to find us someone who knows. Bring them here tomorrow night."

Oscar barked a laugh. "Yeah, right."

"Not kidding."

Oscar paled. Yep, she was serious.

"Langdon has gone to a lot of trouble to fuck up Waylon's life. We need to know why, or we'll make sure he fucks up your life, too." A sour taint lingered in her mouth. She ran her tongue across her teeth and forced a steely glint into her eyes.

Could she follow through if he didn't work with them? Oscar had been a giant pain and had aided Langdon in hurting her and Waylon, but Jason was an innocent and it was his life she was bartering with.

A muscle jumped in Oscar's jaw and his knuckles whitened around Jason's hand. "Two nights."

"No deal," Waylon said. Good. He was with her. She couldn't do this alone, and she would need his support if Jason was caught in the crossfire. "Tomorrow night. Get someone here to talk that you trust won't babble to Langdon after we meet."

"Fine," Oscar said through gritted teeth. "But not here."

Waylon knocked on the top of the car. "My loft. You obviously know where that is. Leave your sister at home. Better yet, don't fucking tell her."

Oscar glared out the windshield. Jason's fear was ripe in her nose. He was a human. No matter how much stolen time he'd spent with Oscar, he couldn't fully comprehend the ways of their people.

Shilo envied him. Somehow, she didn't feel much more superior than Langdon right now.

The couple drove off. Jason must be too rattled to work. When they disappeared from sight, she threw her arms around Waylon.

"Good idea to use them to find out your heritage." She couldn't help the niggling voice in her head that said it couldn't be that easy. But what if it was? "As soon as we have answers, I can finally go home." She released him and put her hand to her forehead, her smile huge. "Sweet Mother, I was starting to think that I might go crazy living in West Creek even without Brynley's help."

CHAPTER 18

*H*er hair brushed down her back as she leaned back, her breasts jutting forward. The exhilaration of making progress toward unearthing Waylon's past, and maybe, just maybe, finding a way to get home for her, had her jumping Waylon as soon as they'd reached the loft.

He was stretched out beneath her. They'd made it to his bed—their bed—before stripping down. She'd shoved him down on it and taken over.

While he'd seemed happy to oblige, the crease between his brows wasn't from effort. She was doing all the work riding him and he was...lost in his mind.

She paused and tipped her head forward to look at him. "What's going on?"

He twitched inside of her. She stayed on him. Connected like this, it was harder to hide from their emotions.

"On the way back, I was pondering my new family and you..."

She sighed and crawled off him. Forget the connection. This might be a while. "And I mentioned that I might be able to go home again after we talk to the person Oscar brings us."

Sitting with her legs folded next to him, he had enough room to roll to his side and prop his hand on his head.

"You miss it," he said quietly.

"Yes. It's my home. *Was* my home. But my family is still there and I worry about them." She missed them.

"We've as good as proved I'm a Covet. Do you think your parents will stand by your side as you officially mate me? They made it clear that was a deal breaker."

"Don't you think we should give them a chance to react without Brynley impressing false emotions on them?"

Waylon sat up. His erection had died, the same with her libido. "I never sensed her casting her ability while I was there. Before we left, that was their real reaction."

Hope and optimism faded. "I can't quit trying to reach them. What if they haven't called because the cell towers aren't working?"

"Reception is spotty at best, I'm sure. Langdon is going to up his game. We're going to have to show our claws before this is over. But when we're done I need to know that you'll still be with me, no matter where we end up."

This again? "I'm here, aren't I?"

"You're here, but you don't want to be."

"Do I want to sit around a bare apartment all day and night with nothing to do but eat and have sex? As amazing as that sounds, no, I don't. I wasn't raised to sit around."

He rolled out of bed and found his pants. How'd they gone from passion to argument so quickly?

He pulled up his jeans. "It's only temporary."

"Is it? If I'm done with Ironhorse Falls, and Covet's secrets are uncovered, then what? You continue at Pale Moonlight and I start applying Mother knows where with my minimal education? The human world isn't partial to 'everything I know I learned from my parents.'"

"Then why'd you leave with me?" He flapped his T-shirt right side out and yanked it over his head. "You thought they'd come after you."

"I came because I love you." Had she expected Mother and Father to jump into their car and speed after her? Maybe, yes.

"Love was never our problem. Trust was." He stomped into his boots. He didn't work for an hour. Where was he going?

"Trust on whose end?" She shoved her hair back and rose to her knees. As gracefully as she could, she crawled to the end of the bed and put her feet on the floor. Fully naked, she slammed her hands on her hips. "I respected your feelings, and I'm here because I stand by you. But what about me? When it comes to my position and my destiny, I'm left standing alone."

His handsome face screwed up. "What are you talking about? I'm right here with you, I take care of you."

"On your terms. When everything's the way you think it should be. But like right now, you're leaving again." A sharp point of fear stabbed her. They were arguing and he was walking out the door.

"I have to work, Shilo. For us."

"Your shift doesn't start until five."

"I have to pick up some groceries and fill the Jeep with gas." A look of disgust crossed his face. "Are you afraid I'm abandoning you, in my own home?"

She went with honesty. "Yeah. I am." Maybe she should've been less bitchy.

"For fuck's sake. I guess we need more than trust. A little respect once in a while would be nice."

Her mouth dropped. Was he referring to the days she'd

spent being manipulated into thinking he was a cheating bastard? Because she'd weathered that like a boss when another shifter would've crumbled.

He shook his head. "When I come home after work, you can decide whether I'm worth trusting or not."

"And you can decide the same," she shot at his back as he walked out.

She puffed out a hard breath. Dammit. They'd had a eureka moment this afternoon and all it had done was dredge up unresolved issues between them.

At least they both agreed on one thing: they'd have to talk when he got home.

~

WAYLON TROTTED into the grocery store. His emotions tumbled through his mind.

What had that argument been all about? There were no tingles in his body. Their emotions had been legit theirs.

On his terms? What had she meant? Being her mate, her companion was nearly impossible when no one else wanted him around and actively tried to prevent his presence.

His mind tripped over one word. Nearly. Weathering the drama in Ironhorse Falls was *nearly* impossible. No, they didn't know what Shilene and Weatherly would do, but if there was a chance that they'd listen to facts and trust that he wouldn't allow Covet to use his birthright to gain control of Ironhorse Falls, then he owed it to Shilo to find out. For no other reason than he was her mate.

He'd never had a family. Uncle Wolf had hid their connection from him and had been nothing but a guardian.

Waylon pondered the thought as he scooted through the produce aisle, grabbing the staples: bananas, apples, carrots, spinach. He couldn't buy meat until he was done with work.

Shifters had excellent metabolism and it took a lot to kill them, but a bout of food poisoning made any species wish they were dead.

Next, he located the peanut butter and bread. None of this was necessary. He usually waited to grab supplies when Shilo could go with him. She was stuck in his apartment all day and going to the store was like a date.

He frowned at the bag of bread he held. He'd used this as an excuse to leave. She'd been right to be worried. They'd argued and before the argument had been done, he'd been dressed and out of the house.

She was right about shit needing to be on his terms. He wanted her to do all the changing and he'd stay the same old Waylon Wolf he was raised to be. When was he going to adapt and change the expectations of his role in life as her mate?

Well, his cupboards were still empty. He ran through self-checkout. The Jeep really did need gas, but it was enough to get home. He'd skip that errand and save it for another day.

Leaving the cart in the corral, he charged out of the store, all the bags in one hand. On his way across the parking lot, he called Christian.

"Can I have tonight off?" Christian didn't like to waste time on pleasantries, especially not during the bar's open hours.

"Cutting it a little close, aren't you?" Waylon could picture Christian arching a dark brow at his Piaget watch.

"There's something I've gotta take care of with Shilo." Waylon didn't want to go into specifics and show off what a thick-skulled dunce he could be. Not that Christian didn't already know. But Waylon had to tell Shilo he was wrong first.

"Take care of it, Waylon. Be back tomorrow."

What a relief. He stuffed his phone in his back pocket and

slipped the keys out of the front of his pants with the other. Opening the Jeep hatch with one hand, he was putting them in when he sensed a presence behind him.

Tensing, he looked over his shoulder.

Oscar's dark gaze glinted. He had a sweater balled over his arm. Someone else approached on his other side. He twisted. Jason, looking much angrier than his typical bartender self.

"What the—" Waylon's words were cut off as two hot pokers speared his torso. Lines of fire cut through his back and abdomen.

Muffled thuds reached his ears. To a human, they probably sounded like a door closing in the distance, but Waylon recognized the noise. Nothing like TV.

Gunshots. But shouldn't it have been louder?

A silencer. Shit. He hadn't been expecting retaliation like this. He should've.

He knees gave away, but strong hands shoved him into the back of his Jeep. Dazed, he didn't fight. The rush of agony through his entire body staggered him. He only wanted to crunch in on himself to see if it'd make the hurt diminish slightly.

He'd never been shot before, but fuck it hurt.

Shot. Oscar. One of the males lifted his legs and folded them into the cargo space of his ride. He punched out with an arm that moved as if it weighed a few hundred pounds.

"Not so fast," Oscar snarled, slapping his hand back. The jostling sent more lightning bolts of agony through his body. "Instead of meeting you tomorrow, I figured I'd just use your bleeding, broken body as bait."

Bullets weren't going to kill him. He just needed to take another breath or two before he could fight back.

No shouts came from the parking lot. It was a busy time

of day. Humans off work, minding their own business. A flurry of activity.

A cool barrel pressed against his temple.

The clatter of a shopping cart in the nearest cart corral made Oscar flinch, the cold metal jumping against his skin.

"Oscar, no." Jason's whisper was ragged. "People are heading this way. We have to leave. The silver will keep him down. Killing him isn't the plan." The hatch slammed shut.

Sweet Mother. They'd hit him with silver?

The wooziness, the raging wildfire of pain in his gut, the sudden onset of weakness. He'd been poisoned and was as weak as a kitten.

The front door opened and closed. One of them had grabbed his keys, and probably his phone. Another door opened and closed.

Heavy breathing reached his ear as he struggled to stay conscious.

"Did anyone see us?" Jason asked. He sounded closer. Was he in the backseat?

"We'll get out of here before they figure out what they saw. Knock him out."

It was now or never. Waylon summoned all his energy to surge over the backseat, but it was the equivalent of swimming through Jell-O. His eyes had barely cleared the top when Jason rammed his fist into his skull, knocking him out.

CHAPTER 19

*A*ny minute now. Shilo paced the floor of the apartment. It was four in the morning and Waylon hadn't come home yet.

Could he have waited until after work to get gas and groceries?

For the one hundred thirty-eighth time, she did the calculation. He was done with cleanup usually no later than two. Groceries for the two of them in a nearly empty store wouldn't take two hours at this time of night. Ten minutes at the gas pump.

Where was he?

She prowled to the front door, around and through the kitchen, treading across every inch of open square footage.

Fifteen minutes ago, she'd tried calling, but it'd gone to voicemail.

She tried again. Nothing.

Was he ignoring her?

Had he…left her?

No. She was at his place.

But he'd been living with her when he'd left the first time. All he'd needed was his Jeep.

The first time. She didn't know whether he'd jetted or not. He was just…not here.

Her gut churned. Her intuition screamed that something was wrong.

Tentatively, she stretched her mind out. *Are you coming home tonight or not?*

She waited.

Nothing.

Waylon?

He could be out of range, which was disturbing enough. Mates could mind speak even when miles apart. But what if he wasn't? What if something was wrong? She'd called him a coward before, but he wasn't. He'd asked for her trust and she'd given it to him.

She charged to the counter and grabbed her phone. Waylon had programmed Christian's number in. She found it and hit send.

Three rings later a grumpy female with a Southern drawl answered. "Whoever this is had better know what time it is."

"It's Shilo Ironhorse. Do you happen to know where Waylon is?"

Fabric rustling drifted over the line. Christian spoke next. "He called and asked for the night off because of you."

"He didn't even work tonight?" Panic clogged her throat.

"No, ma'am. What's going on?" His concern made her feel both better and worse.

"I don't know yet. We had a fight and he hasn't come home yet."

"That's not like him."

No, it was, and that's what scared her. "Sorry to bother you two. Give my apologies to Mabel."

"She can hear everything." Shifter hearing. No wonder

Christian had taken over the phone so fast. "Listen, call me if you find out he's in trouble. And remember, the Guardians always have someone in town."

She passed on her thanks again. Calling the Guardians wouldn't do any good. She had no idea if something was wrong, just a sense of trouble that was vague and unhelpful.

Reorganizing her brain into being proactive, she took stock of her situation. No car. No contacts. No idea what had happened to Waylon.

But she had some money. Waylon stacked his tip money in a safe and he'd gotten her a debit card, just in case she ever got to a point where she wouldn't be a target.

She called a cab. While waiting, she found Waylon's bag and packed supplies. A change of clothing because she didn't know how long she'd be gone. The last apple and the rest of the protein bars. All three of them.

Weapons. Did he have anything? Waylon never carried more than a knife. It hadn't been necessary. If more of a fight was necessary, then they shifted and used teeth and claws.

But that didn't mean others weren't packing, or that she wouldn't run into trouble on her hunt for her mate.

Searching his place gained her nothing more than a folding knife and a utility tool that had fingernail clippers in its mix of options. Better than nothing. Too bad all of Uncle Wolf's guns sat useless in his cabin.

With no weapons, perhaps she should pack in the event one was used on her. She veered into the bathroom and dug out Waylon's first aid kit. She stuffed that into the pack. It took up more room than anything else.

She was going through the kitchen when she stopped at a cupboard by the sink. Waylon's spice rack was inside. She opened the door. A bottle of Morton salt was closest to her hand. Silver poisoning was rare, and usually inflicted intentionally, but she didn't have a gun. And Waylon had said silver killed Uncle Wolf. If he'd gotten into a fight with Langdon's dad, then they had silver-laced bullets.

It might be her paranoia talking, but if hefting salt made her feel more badass, then it was what it was.

The salt was the last item to go into her bag.

The taxi pulled up as she was locking up. She hopped in. "Nearest rental car place."

It would be cheaper to rent a car and comb Freemont than to pay the taxi to drive around for hours.

Because she was going to find Waylon and get answers.

WHAT THE HELL was going on?

Waylon groaned and cracked an eye open. The amount of energy that took almost put him back to sleep.

Darkness. Repetitive bumps jostled his aching and weak body, and the drone of an engine surrounded him.

Was he in the trunk of a car?

He listened hard, reached out with his senses to go beyond the drone of the engine.

"Where'd he say he was meeting us?" Oscar.

Am I in their sedan?

Foggy memories rose of getting jumbled and shoved during a transfer from his Jeep to a trunk. He'd barely come to and Jason and his fist of doom had knocked him out again.

"He said to meet two hours after dawn at the far edge of your land." Jason wasn't sounding as scared as he'd looked when Waylon and Shilo had confronted him, but there was still a quiver in his voice.

The things we do for our mates. Waylon would've snorted at his sarcastic thoughts if he'd had the energy.

"The service road, I suppose, but I don't like meeting him

in the middle of nowhere. But I've got a silver bullet just for him."

Him must be Langdon. Were they going to assassinate their leader?

Why not? Seemed to be a family trait. He vaguely recalled Oscar calling Waylon bait. Was it too much to wish they'd kill each other and leave him be?

"So we keep this one alive until you deal with your cousin?"

"I'm not a maniacal murderer like my dear cousin. Waylon needs to be alive. Langdon will know something's off if he smells death." At least Waylon had that little bit of time on his side. "Sadistic bastard wants to do it himself since the guy messed up his careful plans."

"Trying to use Brynley to turn Shilo on him didn't work," Jason agreed. "Why's Langdon still trying to land her?"

"Because if he interferes with someone else in Ironhorse Falls now, it'd be too obvious. That colony would turn on him. And we can use his preoccupation with Shilo and her mate against him."

For fuck's sake. Like his situation needed even more drama. Oscar and Jason were using him to gain their own form of freedom? Well, it wasn't the worst idea, but he didn't care to take part in it and get killed in the crossfire.

Waylon's eyes fell shut. He'd never been so sick in his life, and he doubted there was a salt molecule to be found in this vehicle. At least not one he could have until he'd served his purpose for their escape.

He was so screwed.

Screwing his eyes shut to keep from groaning, he clutched his belly. Blood had crusted on his shirt. His wounds refused to heal thanks to the silver. Fresh blood continued to seep, smearing his skin and clothing.

When he didn't come home, what would Shilo do? What would she think?

He had a feeling he knew. What else could she think? He'd stormed off after an argument and hadn't returned. History, meet repeat.

And he hadn't gone to work. If she called Christian, his boss would have a whole lot of nothing to pass along, only that Waylon had said there was some shit between him and Shilo. Which would only reinforce her assumption that he'd taken off like a bastard.

New rule if he survived this: never leave Shilo while angry. No good ever came of it.

The car slowed and turned onto a minimally maintained road. Bumps knocked Waylon against all four sides. He threw his arms out to brace himself but passed out before it did much good.

aaaaylooon.

He pried open his eyes. Having given up trying to minimize the impact of the rough road, he rolled with it. At some point, his heart was going to fail, the silver having sapped him of all strength. Did a few more bumps really matter?

Waaaaylooon.

He frowned, or at least thought of frowning because he didn't have the energy for it anymore.

The beautiful voice traveling through his head could be a premortem hallucination.

Waaaaylooon.

But damn, it sounded real.

Sh-shilo?

Waylon! The sharp bark made him wince. *Oh my God, where are you? I found the Jeep abandoned on the side of the highway heading out of town. I've been driving all over with the window down, mentally yelling for you.*

If he'd had a fraction more of his health, he would've laughed. The two idiots who'd abducted him hadn't checked the gas gauge before driving off to Passage Lake with him in the back.

Waylon would've already been delivered to Langdon's doorstep and roasted like the rest of his family if it hadn't been for the Jeep running dry. Oscar had had to wait while Jason literally ran back to town to the get the car.

It'd taken hours. Blessed hours that had been still and quiet while his body fought against the poison in his veins. It had both drained him and saved him at the same time.

Oscar and Jason got me at the... His eyelids drifted shut. He forced them open. If he passed out, he was done for. *Silver-laced bullets. Meeting Langdon. Service road. Edge of Passage Lake. Soon.*

Hang in there. I'm on the way.

Shilo and what army? *Don't come by yourself. I will relay info. Give you proof.*

Yeah, totally. I'll just hang out here and listen to you get killed.

He managed a smile at her flat tone. *Sorry. Was coming back. To you.*

Waylon. The soft caress in his mind was the best he'd felt since he'd been shot.

Did she say she was driving? *Car?*

Rental. I burned your tip money.

What it was there for.

Shilo believed in him. If his situation didn't improve, he could at least die in peace.

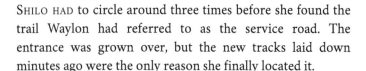

SHILO HAD to circle around three times before she found the trail Waylon had referred to as the service road. The entrance was grown over, but the new tracks laid down minutes ago were the only reason she finally located it.

She stopped briefly to make a call. Another contact

number Waylon had given her. She'd already called them once tonight.

A deep voice answered. "Bennett."

Shilo rattled off the situation and where she was to the Guardian. "So can you help?"

"On our way."

Shilo eyed the trail, seething with determination. "I'm not waiting."

"Didn't expect you to. Watch your back." The line went dead.

No wonder Waylon liked these guys. Few words, even fewer questions, and complete competence—she hoped.

But the Guardians weren't going to make it in time. She had to move before Langdon got his filthy paws on Waylon. The setup to make her mate disappear was too perfect for Langdon to resist.

Shilo eased onto the road. Road was a generous word for it. Thankfully, she'd rented a Jeep. She should've driven out here first thing, but she'd wound through Freemont, over to West Creek and back. Then she'd thought maybe Waylon had headed this way to get answers for good from Passage Lake.

Finding his Jeep sitting abandoned on the side of the road and smelling like absolutely nothing had made her suspicious. She'd gone over every scenario, but not an abduction.

They'd taken her mate. Pumped him full of silver and were making him hurt.

Absent Brynley's mental influence, she hadn't thought she had a strong violent side. She'd always played it down, gone the politico route. She was the negotiator after all.

But they'd taken her mate and she was done with their bullshit in Ironhorse Falls.

She drove until she found a section sparse enough to fit the Jeep. As she pulled off, undergrowth swiped the bottom of the vehicle and branches scratched the paint.

There wasn't enough tip money to cover the damage, but she wasn't going to waste precious seconds worrying about it.

Wedging between two trees, leaving enough clearance to open her door, she parked.

By the time her feet hit the ground, she'd made the decision to stay in her human form. She dumped as much as she could from the backpack, keeping the knives and salt. If she had to shift, she could carry the pack easier as a wolf.

Staying parallel with the trail, she sailed through the woods. Her breath rasped in her ears as she jumped, ducked, and tumbled through the woody terrain. Part of her wished they were meeting on the other edge of Passage Lake, where a few more evergreens grew. They clogged out the bush a little better than the saplings and mature trees she was sprinting through.

But the drive would've been farther, and the land hillier. In this area, she didn't have to climb and worry about cartwheeling off a ridge she didn't expect as much as where she lived.

Didn't mean her glutes and lungs weren't getting a stellar workout. Muscles in her legs burned, and her calves wanted to cramp, but she kept going.

This would be so much easier and faster if she shifted, but the salt was critical. She couldn't risk it.

A myriad of scents assaulted her. She slowed. Waylon's blood hit her like a silver-laced wall.

A familiar voice stopped her. "Do we leave him in the trunk until Langdon gets here?" Jason.

Shilo ground her teeth together. To think she had pitied him instead of considering that he must possess some vicious fortitude to be Oscar's mate.

"No," Oscar answered. "I want to make sure he's visible

when the others get here. You'll need to head into the woods and hide before they arrive. I'll cover your scent."

Jason's anxiety pushed out far enough for her to scent. "I feel so guilty."

"It's okay, baby. We do this and then we'll be gone. My kin will be out of our life."

Was Oscar planning to leave town with his mate? They could've banded together against Langdon. But Oscar likely trusted no one after growing up the way he had.

No, this was no time for compassion. No matter who the victor was, she needed to save Waylon.

Oscar had mentioned others. She was already outnumbered two to one. Langdon never traveled alone. Paulie and Brynley would be with him.

The faint squeak of the trunk hinges reached her. They couldn't be that far away. Shilo slipped around a tree, picking her footing carefully. How close dare she get?

Closing her eyes to fully sense the wind, she calculated her path. Circling to the right, she angled herself to keep her scent from wafting over them. Getting close without being detected was still out of the question. Just a glimpse to see how they were situated before she attacked.

They were stopped in the middle of the road. Langdon might be coming on foot from the other way or following the same path she had. It was possible that they'd see her hiding spot, but she doubted it'd slow him down.

She couldn't underestimate Jason again, but she doubted he was the fighter Oscar was. The acrid stench of Jason's nerves was clear. Oscar hadn't covered the man's scent yet, probably to save energy if he planned a sneak attack on Langdon. The human would have to be a dirty fighter to keep up with shifters. And there was the gun with silver-laced bullets she had to consider.

But she had to try something before the others arrived with their indeterminate numbers.

Carefully, she shrugged off her pack. She ripped her shirt off and tossed it down. Next her shoes and pants came off. She shifted.

"Holy shit, he's not doing well." Jason was peering into the trunk. "Think we should hit him with some salt?"

"I didn't bring any."

Jason had the grace to give Oscar a perplexed look. Shilo agreed with it. Pack that toxic kind of heat and not bring the ability to save yourself from an *oops*?

Idiot.

"It's not like I planned to get blackmailed today," Oscar snapped. "Or to kidnap fucking Waylon Wolf."

"But you carry silver-laced bullets around?" Jason shoved a hand through his blond hair and spun away from the car and the trunk.

Shilo stalked closer, stealthier in her wolf form, braver. She inched closer than she had planned to on two legs.

"Hey." Oscar left Waylon in the trunk. Her mate's pain and blood clogged the air and fed her rage, prodding her to attack without a plan, but she held fast. Jason should be easy enough to subdue. Oscar a little harder.

Jason shook his head and took a few extra steps away. Fatigue weighed on his shoulders. A long night and the stress of stealing her mate and fleeing Oscar's psychotic family must be weighing on him.

A glint of metal from Oscar's waistband caught her eye. He'd shoved the gun behind his back. He'd be the one to attack first.

"Hey," Oscar said again, gripping Jason's shoulders from behind to stop him from getting farther away. "This is my life. You knew that."

"It's just different seeing it than hearing about it.

Different experiencing it." He was going to turn around. She had to act while their backs were to her. In a different world, they could talk it out. Join sides to stop Langdon. But these two smelled rigidly resolute.

Shilo crouched, then launched. Claws dug into the dirt as she flew through the trees, bounding as fast and as far as she could.

Oscar spun around, his hand reaching around his back.

"What—" Jason might sense her, but he was completely unprepared for what to do.

She tore across the distance between them, but it seemed like slow motion. Oscar's arm pausing. His shoulder flexing as he swung his arm around. She might not make it, but all she needed was to clamp her jaws around his neck and he'd go down.

The muzzle of the gun caught a glint of the early dawn sunlight streaming through the dappled canopy. Oscar's eye was squeezing shut to aim. She was going to get plugged. Dammit. This plan could've used more thought, but that would've taken more time, and—

From the trunk, a dark object sailed out and *thunked* Oscar on the head. A boot. His head jerked and the gun fired somewhere over her. The only reason her ears weren't ringing was because of the silencer.

Two more leaps and she tackled Oscar. He careened backward, the gun skittering on the ground toward the car. Jason, who hadn't stepped out from behind Oscar, got pushed down beneath his mate.

She didn't know who the grunt came from, she just ripped into anything her jaws could latch on to. Her fangs scraped across his chin and she snapped her teeth together.

"Fuck!" Oscar twisted and turned, but between her weight on top and Jason's body tangled up beneath him, he couldn't get very far.

She snapped again, catching his shirt. Ripping it, she went for his throat but got bucked off. Jason had heaved up and away, tumbling her and Oscar off him.

She charged again as Oscar flipped to his hands and knees.

Dirt crunched and grass rustled behind her as a heavy object hit the ground. She couldn't spare it any attention. She plunged into Oscar. He threw his hands up to push her off, but she had the benefit of momentum. Knocking him back down, she flipped around to drape over his back. Opening her mouth and aiming, she bit down. Oscar cried out, throwing himself around to toss her off, but he couldn't get enough leverage.

Shaking her head, she ground her jaws together for maximum injury. She sensed movement to her left before a heavy kick landed on her ribs.

She loosened her hold, but snapped down again and whipped her head back and forth. Nausea rose. Another boot hit her ribs. She yelped, but before Oscar could get away, she snapped down tighter than a metal trap. Warm blood welled in her mouth and what normally shouldn't bother her almost made her gag. His desperation was sour.

Her side throbbed, but she prepped for another kick. Jason might've cracked a rib.

Oscar collapsed to the ground, covering the pool of blood gathering under him. A shadow blocked out the sun. Another kick was coming, this one toward her head, and she knew this would be the one to disengage her. She only hoped she had enough wits left to take on Jason. Oscar wasn't going to be quick on his feet.

A muffled shot fell flat in the trees. Jason stalled for a moment, his eyes flaring, before folding to the side. His body hit the ground with a grunt.

Oscar's yell was merely a hoarse whisper. "No!" He

reached for his mate, but the loss of blood and the trauma she'd caused sapped his strength. He went limp under her.

But she didn't let up. Adrenaline pumped furiously through her.

"Get off him," Waylon croaked.

Shilo released Oscar in an instant. He was passed out. Waylon was prone on the ground, his face pale, his socked feet splayed out. He held the gun and miraculously his hand wasn't shaking.

She jumped off Oscar and staggered a few steps. Fire lanced her side, but she was still standing. Waylon was alive and the two other males were down.

That should be enough to keep them both down. She no longer wished to kill the couple. If she were in their position, she would've done the same thing. They were going to have it rough enough if they survived. *I've got salt.*

She ran back to her pack and wedged her head under one strap. Back at Waylon's side, she shifted. Warm air surrounded her and did little to ease the protesting of her bruised ribs.

Waylon was even paler up close. He'd collapsed onto his back, his arms limp at his sides. Dried blood crusted his shirt. His shallow and uneven breathing spurred her urgency. Taking his boots off and falling out of the trunk had nearly robbed him of all life. He was fading fast.

She fumbled with the salt, ignoring the stabs of agony in her side. Dumping a pile in her hands, she rubbed them together. If she happened to brush against a wound, some grains might get inside. Anything helped.

She gripped his hem and ripped the shirt until his front was two panels of material. He was so bloody, she couldn't tell where he'd been shot.

Biting her lip, she poured more salt into her palm and rubbed it all over his torso. His eyes had fallen shut.

"Don't die on me." She hadn't got her mate back just to lose him to fucking silver.

Squeezing his lips together, she made enough of a pocket to dump some grains of salt inside.

He screwed his face up and smacked his lips. "Uck."

It was helping.

"Where were you shot?" Shaking the salt container, she gauged how much was inside. Not quite half full.

"Back. Twice."

Bracing her heels into the ground, she rolled him over.

A low, long groan escaped him, but he didn't fight her. He couldn't offer any help, but she didn't need it.

Peeling the shirt away from where it had stuck to his skin, she searched for the holes. Racking her brain, she tried to recall the rules for silver. Bullets were usually dipped in a silver solution since actual silver bullets weren't practical. He'd been shot twice. Two holes.

She piled salt into her hand and chose a mucky spot on his back that had to be one entry point. The salt acted like an exfoliant as she ground it into his skin, and as soon as the opening was cleared, she plugged it inside of him.

"Fuck me, that hurts." Waylon faced away from her, still too weak to twitch.

She smiled. "Is it just a coincidence that your mouth is the first thing to come online?"

There, the second hole was only a few inches from the first. Were the bullets still inside of him? As long as they took care of the silver, his shifter side could heal around the lead until it could be surgically removed.

She let him relax against the ground as much as he could to recover. And to give her time to think. She'd done it. Waylon rescue, phase one complete.

CHAPTER 21

$\mathcal{T}$he inferno in Waylon's gut hadn't died down. If anything, it burned fiercer. He took it as a good sign. The silver was no longer poisoning him so badly that he was too weak to feel the ravaging his body had taken from the bullets.

Shilo's footsteps were all around him. He blinked into the dirt. Trampled grasses helped prevent him from breathing grit in.

A seedling of strength returned. The salt was negating the effects of the poison and his body was attempting to repair itself, but until he got a few rare steaks inside himself, and the lead out, his injuries would be an obstacle.

He and Shilo had to get out of here. He'd tell her that, but she was likely already on it. She'd tracked him down not knowing who'd taken him or where, and without knowing that he hadn't just walked out on her.

Love swelled, lending a smidgeon of extra healing energy.

He propped his hands under himself and pushed. Amazingly, his body responded, his muscles firing. But getting to his hands and knees was the easy part. His mate was doctoring an unconscious Jason.

In a heartbeat, Shilo was next to him, lifting him to his feet. She wedged a shoulder under his arm. He swayed, remaining standing only because of her strength.

"I fucking love you," he said. The words just poured out of him. He should conserve his budding strength for moving, but after the way they'd parted and his terror that he wouldn't ever get a chance to set the record straight, he had to finish. "I was so scared you'd think I was just a bastard who couldn't take not being right. Or that I didn't understand how much you miss your family. Or how much of your birthright is leading Ironhorse Falls. I mean, I'm beginning to understand and I know you have to try to get your position back. This relationship isn't about what makes me comfortable, it's about us. You're a leader. I'm your mate, and while I might storm off and get groceries if we bicker and yell, I'll always come back. If I don't, you might have to come save my ass again."

She gaped up at him, emotion welling in her brown eyes. She was still nude from the shift, but there was nothing sexual about his declaration. She was everything to him and if they survived this, he wasn't going to be negligent about telling her how important she was to him.

Her free hand caressed his face. He tipped his head into her touch.

"I love you, too. Whether you're Waylon Wolf or Waylon Covet, you're mine." Her shrewd gaze darted to the road. "We need to go."

He listened. Yes, that was a motor and it was growing louder by the second. Oscar twitched. The male would come to soon. He'd be frantic to rescue his own mate. They wouldn't have to worry about them anymore.

With Shilo's support, he got into the passenger side. Much more comfortable than the trunk.

He curled a lip. Stuffed in the fucking truck.

Shilo slipped behind the wheel and handed him the gun and a protein bar. "Eat that. I have two more." She tossed a backpack in the back.

Shilo threw the car in reverse and stomped on the gas. Waylon lurched forward, but caught himself before his head banged the dash. He fumbled with the wrapper and shoved the whole bar into his mouth, surprised he had enough spit left to chew after the salt.

He ripped the remnants of his shirt off. The heft of the gun felt good. Stable. Uncle Wolf's lessons ran through his mind. At the time, Waylon had thought he might use them someday. His future had seemed dark and lonely, the weapons to protect his back a necessity. Then as an adult, he'd set aside his shotgun for a soda gun, and that had been more than okay. He wasn't the type to go looking for violence. But Uncle Wolf had known what Waylon might face in the future. He'd been the only one to know exactly who Waylon was.

Resting the sidearm on his thigh, he glowered into the rearview mirror. He couldn't see Langdon's vehicle yet, but they were coming.

Shilo flew along the trail, the bumps slamming his head against the top of the car. She had the wheel to hold onto and fared better. Waylon braced his hands on the door and dash.

Tiny hairs on the back of Waylon's neck quivered. The engine quit.

With no power, the car rolled to a stop. Shilo turned the key, pumped the gas, hit the steering wheel.

"Fuck!" She craned her head around.

Paulie.

"They're going to be pissed when they find Oscar," Waylon stated the obvious.

Or maybe Langdon wouldn't care. Waylon was the bigger prize.

"Can you shift and run?" She reached over and undid his fly.

Whoa. His healing had reached the point that his groin warmed, like it considered pleasuring Shilo more important than survival. *Wrong priorities, buddy.*

"I think so." He'd have to, but his run wouldn't be full speed.

She grabbed the gun from him and slipped it into the backpack. She got out and changed into her wolf.

As much as he wanted to admire the richness of her coat and the strength in her stance, Waylon opened the door and caught himself before he fell out. All he had to do was shed his pants and shift.

He was glad she was on the other side of the vehicle. The transition sapped a lot of energy and he sagged, his muzzle close to the ground.

Usually, the change flooded his senses with sharp smells, brighter colors, and vigor. Not today. The protein bar was kicking in, but it'd burn off fast.

The motor grew louder.

Over here.

Waylon padded around the vehicle. Shilo held the pack in her mouth. She could probably outrun him like that. She might have to.

I'm not leaving your side. Her voice caressed his mind.

If it comes to it, there's a whole colony depending on you.

Then you'd better run.

A glint of metal far down the path spurred him into a trot. The rough terrain used more of the reserve he didn't have. But as the car closed the distance, he dug deep.

At a run, he traversed the woods. Shilo ran slightly in front of him, guiding him toward her rental car.

Howls broke out behind them. One stood out from the rest. Longer and louder, it welled with rage and frustration.

Brynley. They'd ruined her plans to help her brother and Jason, and her own escape.

The mental attack that came from her was expected, but not the strength. Gone was the finesse, the subtle suggestion. She hammered them with wild and random thoughts.

You're worthless. She's cheating on you. Your family didn't love you. No one loves you. Your colony would rather see you die than lead them with that mutt.

Waylon shook his head. He wasn't inclined to believe one word, but the power behind them made his skull throb.

Shilo dipped her head like she was trying to shake off the nastiness, but it kept coming.

Your mom screamed like the unfaithful pig she was. No one wanted you to lead so they killed your family and tried to kill you.

Now that was just confusing. Was Brynley talking about him or Shilo?

Shilo's just like your cheating mom. She'll spread her legs for Langdon just like your momma did for Layton.

Waylon stutter-stepped.

She's lying. Shilo broke around a tree. He went the other way and kicked up his speed, but he couldn't shake the accusations.

Langdon's the better brother. Your dad hated your mom for what she did.

Waylon skipped a step and nearly face-planted. His speed suffered.

Shilo will mate you and fuck Langdon because you're a loser just like your dad.

Waylon whipped around, his wounds blazing from the sudden change in direction.

Waylon! Shilo circled around. *She's lying. Come on.*

Was she? It made sense. So much damn sense. And it was like she was telling him exactly what he needed to know, but disguising it as a mental mind game.

The tension in the picture. Uncle Wolf's complete abandonment of Covet, and more glaring, his omission of any of Waylon's heritage. Langdon's constant attempts to destroy him in some way.

Waylon was the Covet successor, and since birth order determined the next in line, he had a legitimate claim to Covet Falls.

Not that he wanted it.

Is that true, brother? Could Langdon even hear him?

The wolves flared out around him. Langdon's wolf was dark, much like his own. Brynley and Paulie resembled each other.

Brynley was trembling, her teeth bared. She was close enough that her snarling was loud and clear, but the look in eyes said she'd rather be back helping Oscar and Jason. Paulie's wolf was as proportionately large as he was and streaked with white. He was older than Waylon had assumed.

Langdon padded forward, his amber eyes hard. Deadly. *We are not brothers.* For a moment, relief beat in Waylon, until Langdon continued. *You're nothing but the proof that your mother was a whore.*

Waylon didn't remember his mother, but a growl rattled his rib cage. *I know you and the rest of my family well enough. My mother was either tricked or coerced. Your father was as evil and weak as you are. Honor is true strength.*

Hate rippled over Langdon. *Just how do you think you can trick a shifter into fucking her mate's brother?*

Waylon's gaze shifted to Brynley. *How old were you at the time? Old enough to have your powers?*

Brynley twitched and glanced away for the briefest

second. She'd probably cast a wide mental net and suggested a young, traumatized Waylon forget who he was.

And I bet my parents couldn't escape. Right, Paulie? Except they got me out with enough of a message to save my life. I bet that pissed your dad off, Langdon.

You're a coward like our grandfather. He left when you were born, you know. Your birth drove our family apart.

No, if that were true, Uncle Wolf wouldn't have claimed him in Ironhorse Falls. Had he known what Langdon's father had done? Had it driven him away when he'd predicted his family would rip itself apart?

Waylon bared his fangs. These shifters had destroyed his life. He'd lived alone and unloved until he'd met Shilo, and even then their interference had almost cost him his mate.

Brynley tossed her head back and howled. Paulie charged.

Shilo launched. Waylon's instincts were to stop her, but she was uninjured and the best one of them to take on the bigger shifter.

Brynley sprinted for him, drool dripping off her fangs.

Letting others do your shit like always? Waylon taunted before he twisted out of Brynley's reach.

He leaped on her as soon as she landed. Uncle Wolf's lessons rushed back. *Go for the neck. Pin 'em down. Keep fucking calm, Waylon.*

Waylon pivoted and ducked, fending off the shifter's teeth and claws until he spotted an opening. Brynley was a good fighter, but she hadn't been trained by Uncle Wolf, and she was fighting less than one-hundred percent. Without coming to an agreement, they put on a show. She knew he could've killed her brother and Jason.

He wrestled on top of her and sank his fangs into her neck. Shaking his head, he pinned her to the ground.

She yelped and squirmed, blasting him with doubts that

were so loud and frantic, they didn't make sense. When she went limp, playing her part, he was caught off guard.

A heavy body landed on him. He and the new attacker went rolling. Langdon was first on his feet. Waylon's adrenaline faltered. They faced off. Snarls and yelps spiked the air behind him.

Your mate's losing.

Waylon couldn't risk looking. He had faith that Shilo could handle a male bigger than herself. He'd seen her practice with her parents. She was quick and clever.

But the iron tang of her blood tinted the air.

Waylon bunched his haunches under him, but too late, the telltale tingle along his back alerted him. He lunged and—

Went nowhere.

What the hell?

He strained, but he could not move one muscle. How his friends had been killed was suddenly clear.

What's wrong, brother? Scared stiff?

That's how you got to Charlie and Cass.

Langdon bared his teeth and circled. *If they'd been strong enough, they could've fought it, but that seems to be a common weakness with shifters from Ironhorse Falls. They lack power in all aspects, including their future leader.*

Waylon refused to rise to the bait. He had to think his way out of this.

Waylon pushed against Langdon's influence over him. His body quivered from the effort, but his paws remained rooted in place.

The yelp that cut through the air was Shilo's.

No! He couldn't lose her. Paulie was bigger, but he wasn't as smart. Shilo could outmaneuver him. She had to.

Langdon calmly padded to his side, sniffed his fur, and drove his fangs into Waylon's neck—slowly. Brynley didn't interfere. Her fear of Langdon couldn't be the last thing he tasted.

Sweet Mother, the pain. Langdon's inexorable bite, his canines heading to his carotid—

A blast echoed through the air. Langdon jerked, his mouth falling off him.

Waylon lurched forward, the command to freeze gone. He spun around. Langdon had staggered to the side, red staining his hide. Who'd shot him?

Waylon searched for Shilo. She and Paulie crouched across from each other, growling. The gunshot must've startled both of them enough to separate.

Neither one appeared to be in good condition. Blood dripped from Shilo's mouth and was spattered across her fur. She was favoring her right side and held her front right paw off the ground.

Paulie wasn't in any better shape. His flanks heaved and he was smeared from nose to tail with red. He wobbled like one stiff gust of wind could topple him.

Guardians, Shilo gasped in his head.

Fuck. Yeah.

Before Langdon recovered, Waylon jumped him. He didn't know the extent of Langdon's ability but hoped to distract him from using it if nothing else.

Langdon was quick and agile. As Waylon was about to land on him, the other shifter twisted and rolled. Claws ripped across Waylon's side, but he ignored it and seized the only sliver of an opening he could find. When he struck, he aimed for Langdon's bullet wound and clamped his mouth down on a limb.

Langdon howled and squirmed harder, but Waylon didn't release. Instead, he rolled. His own injuries protested, but Langdon's were fresh, he was disoriented. He didn't move with Waylon, but tried to resist and pull away.

Bone snapped in Waylon's jaws. He released and jumped back to attack again. Another shot rang out. A warning one.

Langdon lifted himself off the ground, his upper body rising before his haunches. He was hurting. At least Waylon had done that much.

Shilo and Paulie hadn't quit growling at each other. Paulie must have realized he couldn't defeat her as easily as he'd assumed, and now Shilo played the waiting game against him.

Waylon inhaled, trying to move in any way possible. The scent of his own blood filled his nostrils. The wound on his neck seeped freely, unencumbered by Langdon's ability.

I guess I overestimated you, Langdon taunted. Waylon couldn't even use his rage to make himself move. *You were never any match against me.*

A male's shout filtered through the trees. Bennett? "To the two male shifters I've never met, you'd better not move a strand of fur."

Langdon pulled his lips back, a snarl ripping from his throat. He darted for Waylon's neck.

A third blast. Langdon hit the ground. Waylon was free.

"I said don't fucking move." Bennett sounded closer than before.

A cluster of snarls resonated behind him. Paulie had used the distraction to attack Shilo.

Time to end this.

Waylon heaved himself off the ground. Langdon hadn't clipped a carotid, but Waylon hadn't had a lot of blood to spare in the first place. He staggered to the backpack Shilo dropped when she went after Paulie. Shifting back to his human for, he collapsed on the ground.

No. Nope. This wouldn't do. He wasn't going to pass out on his female.

He riffled through the bag, closing his hand around the gun. Two silver bullets, that was all he needed.

Shilo, I need an opening.

If she heard him, she didn't respond.

A tall blond man emerged from the trees. Bennett's hard gaze touched briefly on Waylon, then each downed shifter. Langdon panted, but he wasn't moving. Brynley stayed down.

A second Guardian with black hair overlaid with silver appeared like a ghost behind Bennett. Mercury had his rifle trained on Shilo and Paulie rolling around.

Like she sensed Paulie's distraction, Shilo freed herself and darted away. Waylon aimed and shot. Mercury fired at the same time.

Paulie dropped. Waylon hoped the silver-laced bullet at least grazed him. He readjusted, putting Langdon in his sights.

The male rolled up to his haunches and nearly collapsed back down.

"Langdon Covet. You are under arrest by the Tri-Species Syn—" The last word came out a strangle. Bennett stood stiff as the tree next to him.

Waylon's entire body tingled. Mercury swiveled the barrel but froze halfway through.

A dry chuckle snaked through Waylon's mind. *Weak fucking Guardians. Weak fucking government. I don't answer to them.* He swung his head toward Waylon.

Muscles stiff and unresponsive, Waylon was frozen.

He calmed his mind. All he had to do was move a half an inch. He concentrated.

Shilo cleared Paulie's prone wolf and bounded toward Langdon. The effort of trying to freeze her while keeping three others stiff proved just hard enough.

Waylon would've grinned if he could've. *I might not be a*

match for you, Langdon, but the thing that makes a leader strong is the others around him. Before he pulled the trigger, he added, *Or her.*

He squeezed. Langdon hadn't moved out of his sights. The shot hit him between the eyes. Langdon was the one frozen for a split second before he collapsed backward.

Bennett jerked and stumbled back. Mercury shook his head and lowered his rifle.

Shilo loped toward him, keeping her weight off her front right limb entirely. She shifted when she reached him. He folded her into his arms. Sticky with blood, smelling like pain and death, he clung to her.

It was over. His future was more uncertain than ever, but this female in his arms was the center of it.

CHAPTER 22

*W*ith a sated sexual appetite, common sense returned. Shilo blinked around the room. She swatted the slumbering male next to her.

He grunted and wrapped a corded arm around her. "Ten more minutes."

"You said that an hour ago before I ended up naked. We should've left already." She hopped off the floor. Stepping over the clothing they'd shredded off each other, she searched for decent clothing for the meeting.

"What's taking you so long?" Waylon shot her a wolfish grin and darted into the bathroom. She tossed a pair of dirty underwear at him. They bounced off the door as it swung shut, his laughter fading behind the panel.

She smiled to herself. She'd never felt better, and their official mating this weekend would top off her mental state. Not that being with Waylon day in and day out, waking up to him and going to sleep wrapped in his arms, wasn't completely blocking the madness already.

But this weekend was also the powwow. She'd sent Olga's dress with a courier to Ironhorse Falls. Whether she and

Waylon would get to the powwow was not yet decided. They were waiting to see how the meeting today went.

She was Waylon's mate now, it would be irrevocably binding soon, and then her duty would be supporting him while he led Passage Lake into the future. It was like they'd flip-flopped destinies, and she was trying really hard to accept it.

Waylon had sensed how hard it was for her and they'd talked, but there was nothing to do but keep moving forward. She'd love to repair her relationship with her parents, but her sudden position at the side of the Covet pack leader changed the dynamics between them.

The tension and dismay that had radiated through her parents had cracked Shilo's heart. The relief she'd hoped to see in their expressions had only been replaced by more stress. She and Waylon had packed the rest of her belongings that night and left.

Without Langdon's bribes, the human contractors had quit interfering with communications for Ironhorse Falls. Brynley, Oscar, and Jason were the Synod's responsibility. They'd do time, then be free to choose a pack less heinous than the one they were raised in. And Jason would be able to properly mate Oscar.

Mother and Father had messaged to ensure she'd be at the meeting today. They'd even asked how she was doing, but they'd also said they needed time to figure out where their hearts were really at—without Brynley's outside influence.

The contact had been enough to bolster her hopes that they could rebuild their relationship.

Shilo's gaze landed on the shelf full of carvings. Waylon's stunned and honored expression when she'd pulled out the containers of figurines had been worth the restraint it had taken for her not to destroy them five years ago in a fit of hurt and rage.

The house they'd rented in Passage Lake was nice enough. Her crafting took over the living room, including Waylon's carvings knives and early attempts to get back into the habit. They'd work together as they enjoyed cable, wifi, and constant cell service. Ironhorse Falls had the same amenities now, too.

She brushed away her thoughts as she dressed. The meeting coming up was a big one. All the packs wanted to talk to Waylon, and Mother had sent a missive indicating she'd like to attend, with all of Ironhorse Falls' pack leaders.

Was there hope for repairing the tensions between the towns? Passage Lake had been horribly betrayed while under Langdon's control, and Ironhorse Falls had spent generations loathing Passage Lake.

Waylon exited the bathroom. His style of dress hadn't changed. Hanes T-shirt and jeans with boots. She was in a charcoal pantsuit with a pink undershirt. Old habits and all that. Her status as negotiator hadn't totally dissolved. Helping Waylon navigate pack politics and a couple decades of lies and secrets from his kin hadn't been easy.

But they'd made great progress. She and Waylon could walk around town and receive greetings the whole way. That was a first for Waylon. He'd almost retreated to the male who shunned all around him as a form of self-defense, but he'd persisted and she'd encouraged. He still went by Wolf, though, not Covet. She hadn't suggested that. A pack leader had addressed him as Covet and Waylon had snapped, "I'm not a fucking Covet," and that had been that.

"You look so damn fine." Waylon scanned their bedroom and the plastic bins they used for their clothing. "Think I should wear like a jacket or something?"

"Do you own one?" She knew he didn't.

He grinned. "I was kidding anyway." He held out his hand, ushering her out the bedroom and the house first.

They arrived at the courthouse fashionably late—her idea. It was awkward as hell to chitchat while waiting for pack leaders to arrive.

Waylon strode in. He'd ordered a bigger table than the round one they usually sat at. Four packs from Passage Lake and five from Ironhorse Falls, plus her parents. They'd needed room for thirteen to sit.

Waylon pulled out the chair for her. She met Mother's gaze and nearly fell into her seat. Pride shimmered in her eyes. Shilo looked at Father and her lips twitched. The wide-lapelled Western blazer in gray and black plaid was vintage—he'd had it since the seventies, and it matched his pants. Those she'd made for him. His smile was faint but no less proud.

Had she completely misread them the day she'd left her life in Ironhorse Falls behind?

"What's going on?" Waylon asked when they were settled. He never lorded over his people. Their meetings were conversations. The years he'd been the easygoing bartender were obvious as he listened to pack leaders discuss their concerns.

A Passage Falls pack leader spoke, an older female. Myrriah. "We've reached out to Ironhorse Falls like you suggested, and what we heard was..." Several emotions played across the shifter's face, leaving creases at her eyes and her mouth trembling. Loss. "We've heard nothing but story after story of how humans and shifters alike keep their family traditions alive. We talked to one young male who said Shilo had made his mother a dress so beautiful she wanted to wear it on her last day on earth."

"Olga?" Shilo hadn't meant to blurt out the name. Her projects weren't confidential, but they were private.

Mother dipped her head and nodded. "She paraded around town in that dress. She plans to wear it to the powwow and I imagine not long after that, she and her mate will disappear into the wood to go unto the Sweet Mother."

Olga and her mate were going to die together, but Olga had left everything behind and couldn't bear to die without a piece of her history. Shilo blinked back tears. For once, the significance of her ability was clear. She preserved her people's history, allowed them to keep the differences that set them apart from the Langdon Covets of the world.

"We...uh"—Myrriah glanced at the other shifters—"we haven't had the option to celebrate who we are. Several of our shifters fear for their mental stability since Langdon controlled who was allowed in and out of the colony. We need to roam like our people do. We need to find our mates. We need to preserve who we are as we grow as people."

Waylon spoke. "You know that I of all people, with Shilo of all shifters for a mate, agree. So what's the issue?"

Mother stood. She commanded the attention of the room and Waylon wasn't the least bit intimidated. "Weatherly and I have planned on retiring for several years now."

What? Other pack leaders were nodding, but Waylon was just as stunned as her.

Did you know this? he asked.

Not at all.

Mother reached down. Father clasped her hand. "It took centuries to meet my mate and I'd like to enjoy him. My daughter was supposed to take over for me"—she gave Shilo a sad smile—"but it never happened. And I think it's because this was meant to be. Our colonies need to unite."

Waylon's back hit his chair. He gazed around the room. Shilo tried to see what he was seeing, but she had a hard time getting past her own stunned reaction. Retirement? Unite?

"This is the perfect time," Mother continued, her hand still in Father's. "I pass the mantle on to Shilo. She and Waylon mate. Done." Mother turned to address her and

Waylon. "We all want this. We're worn from conflict and we're tired of isolation. We just want access to the same amenities as other shifters."

Weatherly nodded. "Shifters just want to have fun."

Shilo's laughter spilled out of her, but she had a hard time believing Mother's statement. "Truly? Everyone?"

Myrriah's solemn expression didn't waver. "All who are smart feel this way. And I'm already getting requests to send you orders. Starting with whatever a flapper dress is."

An image of the fringed dress rose in Shilo's mind. Her fingers twitched and her heart warmed to be able to contribute something with her ability. Waylon had admitted to her that now that he'd developed a gift, he felt complete. But with her, he was finally whole. She knew exactly what he meant.

But she'd still showed him just how much she craved him —and how it had nothing to do with his newfound ability.

Waylon spread his hands, accepting their proposal. "Why wait? We're all here."

Shilo gasped, her fingers went to her lips. Reasons why they should wait bubbled up, but she'd waited years already. The important people were here.

Father dug a long box out of his pocket. "I had a feeling you might suggest that." Waylon raised a brow, but Father only pushed the box toward us. "I've known you a long time, Wolf, whether we liked each other or not. And without fucking Covet's influence, it turns out, I think you're an okay guy."

"But," Shilo said, "when we came to you after he fought Langdon..."

"The retirement," Mother answered. "We've been waiting for so long, and with no successor because you're dedicated to Passage Lake, well, the news took us off guard."

Waylon lifted the lid off the box. A mating dagger rested

inside. Father had to have had it crafted recently. They'd been busy planning all this, that was why they hadn't been in contact.

As if reading her mind, Father said, "We bought that and a Scamp. I'm taking your mom around the country. It's already packed."

"We'd better not hold you up." Waylon grabbed her hand and pulled them up. "Shilene, would you do the honors?"

For the first time, Shilo saw her mother look at Waylon with more than disgust and bitterness. "I'd be proud to, Waylon Wolf."

Shilo faced her mate. The ceremony was a blur, the cut of the dagger nothing more than a pinch as they mingled their blood and bonded their souls.

Waylon traced his fingers along her cheek. "Shilo…Wolf?"

She smiled. He was asking, but he wouldn't care if she changed her name to something completely different. He was hers and she was his. "Shilo Ironhorse-Wolf. But you can still call me princess."

HAVE you caught this series from the beginning? Check out Birthright if you haven't, yet.

THANK YOU FOR READING. I'd love to know what you thought. Please consider leaving a review for A Shifter's Claim at the retailer the book was purchased from.

~Marie

. . .

FOR NEW RELEASE UPDATES, chapter sneak peeks, and exclusive quarterly short stories, sign up for Marie's newsletter and receive download links for the book that started it all, *Fever Claim*, and three short stories of characters from the series.

ABOUT THE AUTHOR

Marie Johnston lives in the upper-Midwest with her husband, four kids, and an old cat. Deciding to trade in her lab coat for a laptop, she's writing down all the tales she's been making up in her head for years. An avid reader of paranormal romance, these are the stories hanging out and waiting to be told between the demands of work, home, and the endless chauffeuring that comes with children.

mariejohnstonwriter.com
Facebook
Twitter @mjohnstonwriter

Printed in Great Britain
by Amazon